Michael
at the
Invasion of
France
1943

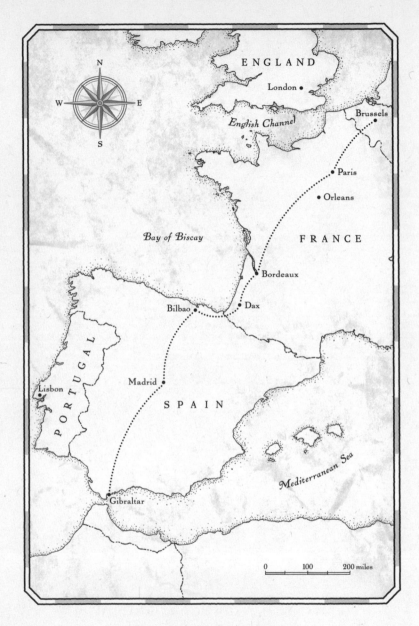

✳ AVIATORS' ESCAPE ROUTE ✳

★ BOYS OF WARTIME ★

Michael
at the
Invasion of France
1943

LAURIE CALKHOVEN

DIAL BOOKS FOR YOUNG READERS

A imprint of Penguin Group (USA) Inc.

For my sisters, Kim Carbone and Leslie Maggio,
with love and thanks

DIAL BOOKS FOR YOUNG READERS

A division of Penguin Young Readers Group

Published by the Penguin Group * Penguin Group (USA) Inc., 375 Hudson Street, New York, New York 10014, U.S.A.
* Penguin Group (Canada), 90 Eglinton Avenue East, Suite 700, Toronto, Ontario, Canada M4P 2Y3 (a division of
Pearson Penguin Canada Inc.) * Penguin Books Ltd, 80 Strand, London WC2R 0RL, England * Penguin Ireland, 25
St Stephen's Green, Dublin 2, Ireland (a division of Penguin Books Ltd) * Penguin Group (Australia), 250 Camber-
well Road, Camberwell, Victoria 3124, Australia (a division of Pearson Australia Group Pty Ltd) * Penguin Books
India Pvt Ltd, 11 Community Centre, Panchsheel Park, New Delhi—110 017, India * Penguin Group (NZ), 67 Apollo
Drive, Rosedale, Auckland 0632, New Zealand (a division of Pearson New Zealand Ltd.) * Penguin Books (South
Africa) (Pty) Ltd, 24 Sturdee Avenue, Rosebank, Johannesburg 2196, South Africa * Penguin Books Ltd, Registered
Offices: 80 Strand, London WC2R 0RL, England

This book is a work of fiction. Names, characters, places, and incidents are either the product of the author's imagination or are used fictitiously, and any resemblance to actual persons, living or dead, business establishments, events, or
locales is entirely coincidental.

The publisher does not have any control over and does not assume any responsibility
for author or third-party websites or their content.

Aviator's Escape Route: Map reproduction Courtesy of The University Press of Kentucky, based on a map by John Hol-
lingsworth, from *Silent Heroes, Downed Airmen and the French Underground* by Sherri Greene Otis, 2001.

Library of Congress Cataloging-in-Publication Data
Calkhoven, Laurie.
Michael at the Invasion of France, 1943/by Laurie Calkhoven.—1st ed.
p. cm.—(Boys of wartime)
Summary: Michael, a thirteen-year-old French-American, watches in fear as the Nazis invade Paris, and is
spurred to become part of the French Resistance movement, defying Hitler, helping American aviators to safe zones,
and delivering secret documents at great risk to his own safety. Includes historical notes, glossary, and time line.
Includes bibliographical references.
ISBN 978-0-8037-3724-2 (hardcover) 1. World War, 1939-1945—Underground movements—France—Juvenile
fiction. 2. France—History—German occupation, 1940-1945—Juvenile fiction. [1. World War, 1939-1945—Underground movements—France—Fiction. 2. France—History—German occupation, 1940-1945—Fiction.] I. Title.
PZ7.C12878Mi 2012
[Fic]—dc23   2011021634

Published in the United States by Dial Books for Young Readers, a division of Penguin Young Readers Group
345 Hudson Street, New York, New York 10014 * www.penguin.com/youngreaders

Designed by Jason Henry
Printed in USA * First Edition
1 3 5 7 9 10 8 6 4 2

---------------------------- ✵ ----------------------------

occupation *noun* 1. The capture and control of an area by a military force.

★ CONTENTS ★

Michael
at the
Invasion of France
1943

★ PROLOGUE ★

BLITZKRIEG

The Second World War began on September 1, 1939, when German troops invaded Poland. They brought with them a new type of warfare—*blitzkrieg*. In the *blitzkrieg*, or lightning war, thousands of German fighter planes and bombers, fast-moving tanks, and ground troops swarmed into Poland at the same time in a massive attack. Poland was forced to surrender in less than a week.

That was the official start of World War II, but it really began twenty years earlier at the end of World War I, when Germany was defeated by

Allied powers that included Great Britain, the United States, and France. The Treaty of Versailles, which was signed at the end of the war, forced Germany to accept blame for the conflict and pay for the damage it caused.

The German people believed the treaty was cruel and unforgiving. The government had to take drastic measures to pay for the war, and the country suffered. People grew hungry and desperate, and they looked for someone to blame.

When a new leader came along who promised to rip up the Treaty of Versailles, the German people supported him. That leader was Adolf Hitler, the head of the Nazi political party, and he was appointed chancellor of Germany in January 1933. He quickly dismantled Germany's democratic government and made himself the dictator of a new, fascist government—a government that insists on obedience to one powerful leader. Hitler also built up Germany's military forces.

Hitler believed that Germans were members of a master race and were superior to all other races. He blamed much of what was wrong in Germany on the Jews and passed laws that discriminated against them.

Hitler's power grew. He made partnerships with other fascist governments and took back land that Germany had lost in World War I. He marched into Austria in 1938 and made it part of the new German Empire, which he named the Third Reich. Next, he took over Czechoslovakia.

The other European countries hoped he would stop there, but then Hitler invaded Poland. France and Great Britain declared war on Germany. Italy entered the war on the side of Hitler. One by one, Norway, Denmark, Holland, Luxembourg, and Belgium fell under the enormous force of the Nazi *blitzkrieg.*

On May 10, 1940, the Nazis entered France. Six weeks later, France asked for an armistice, or truce. The armistice divided the country in two. Hitler allowed the French to keep their own government in the southern part of the country, called the "Free Zone." The French people in the north and those along the entire Atlantic coast were trapped and controlled by Nazi troops.

At first, the French people were too stunned and scared to do anything about the German occupation. Nazi soldiers paraded through their streets and ruled every aspect of their day-to-day lives. Punishments for breaking the rules were fast and terrible. But over time the French people found ways to band together in secret groups and resist the Nazis. That's how the French Resistance was born.

★ CHAPTER ONE ★

The Roundup

July 16, 1942

We heard them before we saw them. Whistles. Stomping feet. Running. The most surprising thing was their voices—French voices, not German, barking orders. Maman, Charlotte, and I left our small, rationed breakfast and ran to the front windows.

Paris policemen were doing the work of the Nazis. They had sealed off the street and were leading families away—old people, children, women and men carrying suitcases. All wearing the yellow star. Even from our third-floor apartment I could see that some were crying. The policemen stared straight ahead, ignoring those who pleaded for information about where they were going and what would happen to them.

Onlookers gawked from the sidewalk. Most seemed embarrassed, but one woman shouted encouragement. "Well done!" she yelled. "Get all the Jews out of France."

We watched the police go from building to building. Soon they were at ours. Boots pounded up the stairs. The metal grille of the elevator gate creaked open and closed. There was banging on a door below us.

"The Grossmans," Maman whispered.

My five-year-old sister, Charlotte, looked at us with round frightened eyes. She played with Sophie Grossman, who was seven, and with Sophie's four-year-old brother, Ernst.

"What can we do?" I asked.

Maman shook her head. "Come," she said, sweeping us toward the kitchen. "Let's not watch."

We stood together feeling weak and helpless. Then there was a knock on the kitchen window. My friend Jacques Dubois from upstairs stood on the fire escape holding Sophie Grossman's hand. I opened the window and he thrust her into my arms.

"Hide her," he whispered.

I looked over my shoulder at Maman. She nodded. By the time I turned back, Jacques was gone. Had he saved Ernst too? I wondered.

Charlotte and I led Sophie, white-faced and trembling, into my bedroom. There was no need for words of instruction. Charlotte patted Sophie's arm and then the little girl burrowed her way to the back of my closet.

Maman nervously paced in the living room. She took Charlotte by the shoulders and peered into her face. "No one must know Sophie is here," she said. "Do you understand? It will be very bad for all of us, especially Sophie, if anyone finds out."

"Jacques knows," Charlotte said, her lower lip trembling.

"Yes, but no one else," Maman said. "If anyone asks, we have not seen her. Do you understand?"

Charlotte nodded.

"Come, let's sit." Maman settled on the couch for a moment and then jumped to her feet, turning to me. "Michael, do you have anything to hide?"

My eyes widened with surprise. I didn't think Maman knew about my secret activities. "No," I answered.

She sighed and then sat again.

Seconds later, there was a knock on our door. "Open up. Police."

Maman smoothed her skirt, nodded to me and to Charlotte, and then crossed to the door.

"Bonjour, Madame Durand," a policeman said.

"Bonjour, monsieur," Maman answered coolly. She didn't ask how he knew her name.

"The Grossman children," the policeman barked. "Have you seen them?"

Maman opened the door wider to show him we had nothing to hide. "Are they not with their parents?"

He didn't answer, only consulted a paper. "They play with your daughter?"

Maman drew herself up. A look of disgust came over her face. "Who told you that?" she demanded. "Not with Jews. My daughter does not play with Jews." She spat the words. I couldn't believe they were coming out of her mouth. She smoothed her skirt again and spoke more calmly. "We've finished our breakfast, but would you like a cup of coffee?"

The policeman's eyes swept across the room, settling for a moment on the photographs of Papa and my brother, Georges, in their French army uniforms. He knew our name. Did he also know that Papa was with the Free French in England? That Georges was a prisoner of war in Germany?

Perhaps it was Maman's offer of coffee. Perhaps it was her ugly words. For whatever reason, he didn't search the apartment but only thanked us for our trouble and went on his way.

I collapsed on the couch and wondered what would happen next.

The police pounding on the door reminded me of the first time our street was sealed off and searched. It was two years ago. That time, it was my brother, Georges, who was in hiding. The Germans found him and threw him in a truck. We never saw him again.

It happened a few days after the Nazis marched into Paris in June of 1940. Our government had fled south, and we'd received a telegram from Papa telling us that he'd evacuated from Dunkirk with the British and was in London. His only question—where was Georges?

Maman had wanted us all to go to America when the Germans swept through Norway, Denmark, Holland, and finally Belgium. We visited her family on Long Island, New York, every summer.

"The children know the language. They can go

to school. America needs engineers too," she had said to Papa. "You can get work."

"A Frenchman's place is with the military now," Papa answered. "The Nazis will never get past the French army. They'll be stopped at the border. You'll see."

My eighteen-year-old brother, Georges, agreed with Papa. He joined the army too. He left Paris in his new uniform, marching confidently. He laughed at Maman's fears. "France has the best army in the world," he said. "We'll have the Nazis on the run in no time."

But it was Georges who was on the run, not the Nazis. The Nazis smashed through the French lines and swept across France. The French army retreated. Three weeks after Georges marched away, he was back. I woke up to a city that was eerily quiet. The air was filled with thick black smoke. I opened my window and within minutes my face and hands were coated with black soot. I thought the Germans were trying to choke us with it, but I found out later that the French army had set Paris's fuel-oil depots on fire to keep them out of enemy hands. I found Maman in the living room with Georges—his uniform torn and dirty.

They were both crying. The Nazis were just a few miles from the Paris.

The next morning, we woke to the sound of loudspeakers from German trucks warning us to be calm and orderly. Nazis swarmed all over the city. They tore down the French flag and replaced it with their ugly swastika. It hung from the Eiffel Tower, the Arc de Triomphe, and every public building in Paris. It made me sick to see it. It made me sick to hear their ugly German voices telling us to do what we were told.

A few days later, the Gestapo, the German secret police, sealed the streets leading to ours. They searched the entire block, apartment by apartment, and arrested the men of military age. Maman had taken Charlotte to the market to try to find some food. As soon as Georges and I realized what the Nazis were doing, he ran to hide in the cellar.

I was alone when the Gestapo burst into our building. They didn't wait for the elevator. I heard their boots pounding up the stairs. I nearly jumped out of my skin when they knocked on the door.

"Open up!" a German voice demanded.

CHAPTER TWO

The Flame of Resistance

June 1940

O pen up!" the German voice demanded again. The Gestapo didn't wait. I was reaching for the knob when the door burst open. They barked words at me in their ugly German accents. I stammered that Georges and Papa were not here. "Georges is American," I said. "Half American. He's not a soldier." In 1940, Germany was not yet at war with America. I thought that would help.

They pushed me aside and went from room to room, searching in closets and behind doors and even under beds.

My mouth went dry when I realized what they would find in my bedroom. Georges had thrown his uniform away, but I had pulled his army shirt out of the trash when no one was looking. I wanted to wear it. It reminded me of Papa. I thought it would make me feel strong.

They found nothing in Georges's room. Then they opened the door to my room. The shirt lay on my bed where I had left it, tangled in the bed-clothes.

The Gestapo turned to me with a sneer. "Where is he?" he demanded.

I stared at Georges's torn and dirty uniform. Why had I not thought to hide it?

"Where is he?" the Nazi yelled.

My voice shook. "He left Paris. He went south."

He grabbed my collar and pressed his face into mine. "Tell me where he is or I'll arrest you too," he snapped.

"I don't know," I said. "I don't know."

He threw me aside, but they kept searching. When they finished with the apartment, they went to the roof, and then to the cellar. Of course they found Georges, and they wouldn't even let him say good-bye. I watched from a window while they shoved him into the back of a truck.

How would I tell Papa? Georges was Papa's only son for eight years before I came along, and he was always Papa's favorite. They were a team, the two of them. Together they went off on adventures and camping trips and took the train to Uncle Henri's farm to help bring in the harvest. I was never included. I was never big enough or strong enough to join in. It felt like Papa never even saw me.

I so desperately wanted to be included. There were times when I thought I might win Papa's favor. When I was five and joined the Boy Scouts, I was sure he would finally notice me. I stood by the front door all afternoon in my uniform, waiting for him. Finally, he opened the door. I stood straight and tall and raised my hand in the Boy Scout salute.

"Papa, I am a scout now!"

"That's nice," he said. He greeted Maman and then sat in his chair with the newspaper.

I tried to tell him about my scout meeting.

"Not now," he said. "I'm trying to read the paper."

I sat on the edge of the sofa and waited for him to finish. He didn't look up until the door opened and Georges rushed in.

Papa folded his newspaper and let it drop to

the floor. "Georges, how did the math test go?" he asked.

Georges sat next to me and talked about his test. Together the two of them laughed and joked as if I wasn't even there. Unseen, I trudged to my room, ripped off my scout uniform, and stomped on it. Maman came in and held me, but that wasn't what I wanted then. I wanted Papa.

Later, they argued and I heard my name. After that, Papa talked to me sometimes and even let me tag along on some of his outings with Georges, but I knew it was only because Maman made him. The only time I ever really drew Papa's full attention was when I had done something wrong.

This was a big wrong—the biggest. I should never have pulled Georges's uniform shirt out of the trash. Later, Maman tried to assure me that the Gestapo would have found Georges even without the shirt. But I knew it was my fault, and Papa would think so too. If we survived the war, if I ever saw Papa again, he would hate me for this forever.

Maman went to every German office she could find to plead for Georges's release, but it was no use. He was a prisoner and would remain one until the war was over.

We were trudging home from one such attempt when a man said that Marshal Pétain was on the radio. We crowded into a café to hear him. While Nazi soldiers paraded through the streets taking pictures like tourists, we listened to the marshal tell us that he was the new leader of the French government.

"I give France the gift of myself to ease her troubles," he said.

People seemed to relax. Marshal Pétain had saved France in the last war with Germany in 1918. He was a hero. *He'll drive the Germans out of France,* I thought, *like he did in the Great War.*

Instead, Pétain told us about his terrible deal with Hitler. He announced that he had asked for an armistice—a truce. France had not been defeated. France had given up.

In exchange for his surrender, Marshal Pétain got to keep a portion of southern France while the Nazis took over the rest of the country, including Paris. They called the south the Free Zone, but that wasn't true. Pétain was a German puppet.

The Nazis took over our radio stations and our newspapers. They wanted to control everything we read and everything we heard, but that didn't stop Maman and me. The day after Pétain handed France over to the Nazis, Maman and I listened to the English news on the BBC hoping for news of Papa. I fiddled with the dial, trying to find the signal amid the static. To our surprise, we heard a French voice. He said he was General Charles de Gaulle. He was in London and he had not surrendered.

"France has lost the battle; she has not lost the war," he said. He spoke of the need to keep fighting and invited all Frenchmen in British territory to join him.

"Papa must be with him," I said. "Papa has not given up." I kept my hand on the dial, turning it when the static got too loud.

The general continued. "Whatever happens, the flame of resistance must not and will not be extinguished."

I whispered the words to myself. "The flame of resistance must not and will not be extinguished." Perhaps Papa would forgive me a little bit for Georges's arrest if I helped to keep that flame alive. I was sure that he was doing the same thing in England.

I looked at Maman. *"Vive la France,"* I whispered.

She took my hand. We both had tears in our eyes. "Yes," she said. "Long live France."

I slept easier after hearing de Gaulle's speech. Then, a few mornings later, I woke to pounding on the door. I stumbled out of bed and met Maman and Charlotte in the hall. We held each other, fearing the worst. Was the Gestapo here to arrest me for lying about Georges? Then I heard my name.

"Michael! Michael!"

The voice sounded desperate, almost hysterical.

"It's Pierre. Please let me in. It's Pierre."

We ran to the door and found my friend Pierre Corbin. He and his family had fled south, along with most of Paris, when it became clear that the Nazis would invade the city. I thought he must have made it to the Free Zone. But he was at our door with torn clothes, dried blood on his cheek, and wild eyes. Tears ran down his face. Maman pulled him into the apartment and into her arms.

"They're gone," he wailed. "I've lost them."

Maman led him to the sofa. He hobbled like an old man. Maman rocked him in her arms until his sobs slowed enough for him to speak. "The roads were so crowded with refugees that it took a whole day to go just a few miles in the car," he said. "We ran out of gas. We couldn't buy any. There was no food to buy, no hotel rooms anywhere. We slept one night on the side of the road and then started walking. There were thousands of us—so many that we could hardly move."

Pierre shook his head. "German planes swooped down and fired machine guns at us to clear the roads for their tanks and their soldiers," he said. "There was panic. I tried to run but I got knocked down. So many people running that I couldn't get up again. I lost sight of Maman and Papa and my brothers. I looked and I looked, but in the chaos . . ." His voice trailed off. His eyes stared at me, unseeing. I could tell he was watching that moment over and over again in his mind.

"There were bodies," he whispered. "After the Germans raced through, I saw them. Facedown. Shot. Trampled. I didn't turn them over. What if—" He couldn't bring himself to ask the question. He was silent for a long while.

"I didn't know what to do," he said finally. "I decided to walk back to Paris. I hoped my family would be home, waiting for me." The tears started to fall again. "They're not there. No one is there. I don't know where they are."

Even though it was a warm summer morning, Pierre couldn't stop shivering. Maman wrapped him in a blanket and got him to lie down in my bed. She whispered to him until he finally fell asleep. That night he woke up screaming for his mother. He did that night after night.

★ CHAPTER THREE ★

Verboten

July 1940

We visited Pierre's apartment every day, hoping to find his family. He trembled whenever he saw a Nazi. I learned to pull him into doorways when I heard them coming. Pierre was not alone in losing his family. The most popular section in the *Paris-Soir* newspaper was the "Missing Persons" column. Thousands of people had gotten separated from their families in the mad panic. Even little children were found wandering alone.

It was weeks before Pierre's whole family was together in Paris again. His two older sisters were the first to arrive. Pierre fell into their arms when they showed up at our door looking for him. They held each other and cried for a long time, but none of them had news of their parents.

Jacques moved back to the family apartment with his sisters, and I kept up my habit of checking every day to see if the rest of the Corbins had returned. One day his concierge greeted me with a wink and a smile.

I didn't stop to talk to her. I raced up the stairs.

Pierre opened the door and his whole family was inside. Mr. and Mrs. Corbin kept hugging Pierre and his sisters and even me. There was a feast spread out on the table—meats and cheeses and cakes and chocolates—foods I hadn't seen since the Germans arrived. Everyone was laughing and crying and eating and hugging all at the same time.

Finally I learned that Mr. Corbin had been put to work by the Nazis. While he was searching for his children, they discovered that he spoke perfect German as well as French. It had taken him this long to convince them to let him and Mrs. Corbin return to Paris, but they had driven him home and rewarded him with the makings of this reunion feast.

The Nazis were on their best behavior in the early days of the Occupation, but they never let us forget who was in charge. They hung an enormous banner reading GERMANY IS VICTORIOUS ON ALL FRONTS across our parliament building. They goose-stepped down the Champs-Élysées, our finest avenue, singing "We Are Marching on England." German military music blared from French radio.

There were posters all over Paris, trying to brainwash us into believing the Nazis were good. One was a picture of a smiling German soldier giving out jam sandwiches to French children while they stared at him like he was Father Christmas. The caption read: "Abandoned citizens, trust in the soldiers of the Third Reich." Other posters used ugly drawings to blame the English and the Jews for the war, but most of the posters began with the Nazi's favorite word: *verboten.* Forbidden.

It was *verboten* to walk down the street between nine o'clock at night and five o'clock in the morning. It was *verboten* to enter cafés and movie houses that the Germans took for themselves. It was *verboten* to refuse German money. It was *verboten* to help escaped prisoners, especially English prisoners. There was a warning beneath that poster, written in big bold letters and underlined twice: ON PAIN OF DEATH.

Even though we were surrounded by enemy soldiers, some things got back to normal—or what we began to think of as normal. They reopened the banks, the post offices, and the *métro*, our subway train. French policemen went back to work, and in July my school reopened.

Pierre, Jacques, and I walked to school together that first morning. I told them about General de Gaulle's speech. I had memorized some of the words and repeated them now. "The flame of resistance must not and will not be extinguished," I said. "We have to resist. It's our duty to become soldiers for France."

"Let's be a resisters club," Jacques said.

"I already did something," I told him.

"What?" Jacques asked.

"A *boche* asked me for directions to Napoleon's Tomb yesterday, and I gave him the wrong ones," I said proudly. It was the first time I used the word *boche* out loud. It was a slang word for the Nazis that they especially hated. "I sent him in the exact opposite direction."

Jacques laughed. "My *papa* won't change our clock," he said. "We're still on French time."

The Germans had told us to move our clocks to Berlin time—the official time of the Third Reich. "Good idea," I said. "What else can we do?"

Jacques looked over his shoulder to make sure no one was within listening distance. "We could tear down their posters."

"Yes! Let's do everything that's *verboten*," I said. "We have to remind people that there are still Frenchmen fighting for France. Not like Marshal Pétain."

"We could write messages on walls and leave notes behind on the *métro*," Jacques added.

The two of us were getting more and more excited, but Pierre was quiet. When he finally spoke, his words were like a bucket of cold water poured over our heads.

"What's so bad about Pétain?" he asked. "My father supports him. He says it's best to go along."

"Go along?" I gaped at him. Some French people thought fascism was better than democracy and welcomed the Nazis, but I was shocked that someone I had known practically my whole life could say such a thing.

"England forced us into war, not Germany. Why should we fight for England? Germany is our partner now," he said.

"You want the Germans to be in charge of France?" Jacques asked. He seemed just as stunned as I was.

"Better the Germans than the English," Pierre said. "Hitler and the marshal will make sure the new French state will be better and stronger than your republic ever was."

"The same Hitler whose troops machine-gunned innocent people on the roads of France?" I asked.

Pierre struggled to find an answer, then he shrugged. "Sometimes civilians get caught up in war. My father says we should have kept our heads and never tried to flee Paris. The Germans did nothing to harm the people who stayed behind."

"They arrested Georges," I said.

Jacques changed the subject. "America is going to enter the war, and they'll beat the Nazis."

I was considered the expert on America since I was half American. I nodded, expressing a confidence I didn't really feel. "America always wins," I said fiercely. "Always."

Pierre snorted. "Americans are only interested

in their precious dollars." He didn't look me in the eye. "Americans are greedy," he said. "They don't care about France."

I was astounded. Pierre was quoting German lies as if they were truths. Did he really believe them or was he just afraid? I opened my mouth to argue, but Jacques signaled me to be quiet. Already people were being encouraged to turn in their neighbors to the *Kommandantur* if they did anything against the rules. Would Pierre do such a thing to his best friends? We walked the rest of the way to school in silence.

When we got to our classroom, our desks were open. Our tutor, Monsieur Declos, sat at the front of the room looking sad and tired.

Jacques picked up a book. "Someone's gone through our things," he said.

I flipped through my history book. Some pages were torn out. On other pages, new typewritten sections had been pasted in over the original text. I scanned the section on the Great War and I gasped. The book had been changed to read that France and its Allies had won a shameful victory over Germany, one that the glorious Third Reich, under Hitler's leadership, would set right.

I wondered how many men and how many

hours it had taken to do this. Did all the history books in France now blame us for the last war? Did they all celebrate Hitler?

I looked my teacher for an explanation. He simply stared straight ahead.

The Nazis had rewritten history.

★ CHAPTER FOUR ★

Liberty, Equality, Fraternity

September 1940

Monsieur Declos said little about the changes in our textbooks that first morning. He called us to attention and began teaching. We fell into our old school routine, but I noticed in the coming weeks that we had no history lessons. I guessed that Monsieur Declos could not bring himself to teach Nazi lies.

One morning, we arrived in our schoolroom to see France's motto—*liberté, égalité, fraternité*—in big letters on the blackboard. For once Monsieur Declos did not have to tell us to be quiet and take our seats. We knew something was about to happen.

"France has a new motto," Monsieur Declos said.
We stared at him with blank expressions.

"Marshal Pétain—the great savior of France—has done away with 'Liberty, Equality, and Fraternity.'" He stood and put a big chalk mark through the words. "Now we have 'Work, Family, Country.' Do you understand the difference?"

No hands were raised.

"There is no place for liberty in the new France," our teacher said sadly. "Liberty has been replaced by slave labor. Fraternity, with family. Do you know why?"

Monsieur Declos answered his own question. "In a society in which a man is only loyal to his family and his country, he will readily turn in his neighbor to the *Kommandantur*."

Stefan Duval, a boy who admired the Nazis, got to his feet. "If my neighbor is doing something against the government, then it's my duty to turn him in," he said. "The marshal knows what's best."

"Pétain and Hitler want blind obedience. You can only have that in a country in which there is no equality," our teacher said. "The new job of the French is to produce goods and soldiers for the Third Reich so that Adolf Hitler can go out and conquer more countries."

Stefan stormed out of the room. Pierre pushed his chair back as if he was going to join him, but he didn't. Jacques and I exchanged excited looks. Here was someone who was not afraid to speak for France! Monsieur Declos was keeping the flame alive.

The next day Stefan swaggered into class wearing the dark shirt, beret, and badge of the Young Guards, a fascist club that trained boys to be Nazis. He didn't openly threaten our teacher, but his meaning was clear.

Monsieur Declos ignored the threat. He continued to speak out against the Germans and Pétain.

Until the day he disappeared.

We arrived at school one morning to find a new teacher sitting at Monsieur Declos's desk. We filed into the room and stood behind our desks. He stood, raised his right arm in the Nazi salute, and greeted us with a very loud *"Heil Hitler."*

Stefan answered the salute with one of his own. *"Sieg Heil,"* he yelled. "Hail victory."

Their words sent a chill down my spine. Our new teacher locked eyes with one boy and then another, waiting for them to respond as Stefan had. No other class in school had been asked to do such a thing. Were we being punished for

Monsieur Declos? I watched the boys in my class surrender one by one and raise their arms in the Hitler salute. Most dropped their eyes to the floor when they did so.

Pierre raised his arm and muttered Stefan's words.

Anger bubbled inside me. It made it even worse that a Frenchman wanted us to salute the enemy. Were the boys around me cowards, or did they feel the same way as Stefan and Pierre?

The teacher made his way around the room. My anger turned to panic the closer he got to me. Jacques caught my eye and shook his head. He would refuse. Would I?

I held my breath as the teacher's eyes landed on Jacques. My friend looked the man right in the eye, but did nothing. The teacher's eyes bored into Jacques's, waiting. Slowly, without blinking, my friend brought his right hand to his forehead and saluted in way of the French and the Americans. He said nothing.

I moved next to Jacques, facing my teacher, and raised my right hand in the French salute. I waited for yelling. I waited for us to get thrown out of class. A few of our classmates joined us.

Our new teacher slammed his hand on his desk

and started toward us. His face was mottled with rage. My hand shook, but I kept it in place.

The teacher had just reached Jacques when the door to our classroom opened. The head of the school stood there, quietly watching. His question was for the teacher. "Have you not started class?" he asked. "We have a strict schedule here."

"Of course." The teacher turned on his heel and walked back to his desk. "Take your seats," he barked. "Stop this nonsense and get to work."

I dropped into my seat and looked over at Jacques with a relieved smile. Our resisters club had just had a victory.

We were never asked to salute the Nazis in school again. Over the next few weeks, we tried to find out what had happened to Monsieur Declos. Some said he had been sent to prison. Others that he had been shot by a firing squad. We never found out for sure. Jacques and I continued with our secret work. We tore down German posters when we could, wrote *Vive la France* and *Vive General de Gaulle* on walls, and refused to speak to the Germans. We kept the flame alive.

★ CHAPTER FIVE ★

Long Live France!

July 1941

One Saturday, about a year into the occupation, Jacques and I planned our first big mission. We wrote messages like "Resist the Nazis" and "Long live France" on a hundred small pieces of paper. We cut and folded them into V's for victory, filled our pockets, and set out for the Colisée, one of Paris's biggest movie houses.

We got to the Champs-Élysées exactly at noon, right in time for the daily Nazi parade. An officer on a horse was leading a fancy unit down Paris's most famous street to the Arc de Triomphe. They goose-stepped in perfect unison.

"Don't look at them," Jacques said.

I turned my back and so did he. Nearly everyone on the street showed the Nazis their backsides, and shopkeepers closed their metal shutters with a clang. It was a small thing, but it made us feel better.

After they passed by, Jacques and I crossed the street to the theater, handed over our money, and made our way to the first row of the balcony. We heckled the German newsreels.

"Propaganda!" I yelled.

"German lies," Jacques added.

The Gestapo hung around public places in civilian clothes spying on people. I studied the moviegoers around me. Was that man in the black coat Gestapo? I wondered. What about the woman in the gray suit? I didn't want to be too close to a Nazi when I carried out my mission. Getting caught in an "act of sabotage" would mean severe punishment, maybe even prison.

An hour into the film, Jacques leaned over and whispered, "Ready?"

I nodded and reached into my bulging pockets. I filled both hands with my paper V's. All my muscles tensed. "Ready," I answered.

I whistled the Morse code signal for the letter

V—three short toots and then one long whistle. We jumped to our feet and ran, flinging our papers off the balcony to the people in the seats below.

"Long live France!" I yelled.

"Long live General de Gaulle!" Jacques added.

Some people began to clap but there was also shouting and then a German voice from somewhere behind us. *"Halt!"* it yelled. *"Halt!"*

We kept running, throwing our paper V's until our pockets were empty. We ran down the stairs, through the lobby, and out the cinema's front doors. We raced all the way to the corner before a stitch in my side made me stop.

No one seemed to be following us. I leaned over, clutched my stomach, and tried to slow my huffing and puffing. Jacques was laughing so hard he could hardly breathe. He had to hold on to my shoulder just to stand.

I started laughing too. I imitated the Nazi who had yelled at us. *"Halt!"* I said. *"Halt!"*

Jacques laughed even harder. Tears ran down his face.

Two Nazi soldiers passed us, smiling at the fun we were having. Suddenly I remembered I could go to prison for shouting the words *Vive la France*. I was done laughing.

Jacques straightened and waited for them to pass. He reached out to shake my hand. "The flame of resistance," he said.

I gripped his hand firmly. "Will not be extinguished," I added.

We had done it. We had reminded everyone in that movie theater that there was still hope for France. I couldn't wait to see Papa after the war and tell him all about it.

Jacques and I wanted to do more and more, but it was hard to plan resistance missions when we were hungry and cold. The first winter of the Occupation was the coldest and snowiest Paris had ever seen. The second began just the same. The Nazis sent all the fuel to Germany. We only had enough coal to heat the kitchen for a couple of hours a day. Gas for cooking was scarce, and the electricity went off without warning. We wore everything we owned, stuffed newspapers into our clothes, and still shivered. The only warm places in Paris were Nazi offices and apartments.

On the coldest nights, Maman, Charlotte, and I went to the *métro* to sleep in the underground passages where it was a bit warmer. We could feel the temperature change as we walked down the stairs into the subway tunnels. People piled blankets on the floors. The ones who got there first set up camp against the white tile walls. The rest of us would pick our way through the families, looking for an empty spot on the floor. It was so dark that there was a danger of slipping off the side of the platform and onto the train tracks if one got too close to the edge. The trains no longer ran at night, but it was still dangerous.

We huddled for warmth in the dark, trying to ignore the noises and the smells of the people around us and sleep as best we could.

In the beginning people spoke openly against the Nazis, but then the *boches* caught on. Soldiers showed up. If someone was too loud, or spoke of something *verboten*, the soldiers turned a bright flashlight on them. Maman, Charlotte, and I would lie on the hard floor, wrapped in blankets, and try to sleep.

In the afternoons after school, I sometimes brought Charlotte to another warm spot—the monkey house at the zoo. One of the monkeys began to recognize Charlotte. It would jump up and down in front of us, screeching and making comical faces. Charlotte would imitate it, giggling like crazy. Eventually, they would both quiet down and take a nap. The monkey curled up in a tree, and Charlotte curled up in my lap.

Paris had become a cage and the Nazis our zookeepers. Did the monkeys hate me the way I hated the Nazis? Did they dream of escaping too?

The Nazis grew meaner and meaner. We never knew when one of them would turn on us for the smallest offense.

One day Jacques and I were walking down the street when two soldiers came up behind us. "Make way," one of them yelled.

I didn't move fast enough for him. He gave me a kick, knocking me into the street. A German truck almost hit me, and then the same Nazi yelled at me for blocking traffic!

"Dirty *boches*," Jacques muttered.

The one who had kicked me turned on his heel and slapped Jacques across the face. My friend fell to his knees, clutching his cheek. Blood collected at the corner of his mouth.

The soldiers continued on their way, laughing.

Jacques got to his feet with tears in his eyes. Both hands were in fists. "Dirty *boches*," he yelled. "Nazi pigs!" This time, the soldiers paid him no mind.

* * *

Food was an even bigger problem than the cold and Nazi anger. Shortly after they arrived, the Nazis made us line up on playgrounds to get ration cards according to our age. Maman needed pink, yellow, and orange coupons to buy potatoes, bread, cheese, vegetables, and meat. Food prices doubled and then tripled. Maman stood on lines for hours, and half the time the food ran out before she got into the store. We were always hungry.

After she spent nearly every penny we had in the bank, Maman sold jewelry and other luxuries in order to buy food. A black market sprang up, which was even more expensive than the shops.

The public gardens, once filled with spring and summer flowers, were plowed and planted with beans and cabbages, and in the spring we made a small garden on the roof. Of course, the Germans took everything they wanted and ate it themselves or shipped it to their precious "fatherland."

One day, seeing rabbit on a menu posted outside a restaurant, I got an idea for a business that could see us through the hungry times. Papa always said a man took care of his family, and now I had thought of a way to do that. My uncle Henri and aunt Jeanne had a farm to the west of Paris.

They kept rabbits. I talked Maman into going to visit them with the idea of trading something for a few of their rabbits.

"Where are you going to keep rabbits in the middle of Paris?" Maman asked.

"In the bathtub," I said.

She didn't like the idea.

"We don't use it to bathe anymore," I said. It was true. Soap was one of the first things to disappear from the stores, and we didn't have enough fuel to heat hot water for baths.

"A good female rabbit can have ten babies every three or four months," I said. "We can sell or trade them for whatever we need."

"Do you even know how to take care of rabbits?" she asked.

"Uncle Henri will teach me," I said.

It took some convincing, but finally she agreed. The rumblings in our stomachs helped to convince her.

One Saturday we took the train to the country. Uncle Henri and Aunt Jeanne were happy to see us. They were even happier to get a stash of prewar coffee and the black-market sugar Maman had hidden under the false bottom of her shopping bag.

My uncle roared with laughter when I told him what I wanted. He had hated the Germans ever since the last war, and now that both of his sons were being held captive in Germany, he hated them even more. "Rabbits in the bathtub," he said. "That's a new one. But it'll work!" His eyes lit up as he chose the best rabbits for me— two females and one male. One of the females was almost ready to give birth. Uncle Henri told me everything I needed to do to take care of them.

"You'll have more rabbits than you know what to do with," he said.

Maman wrinkled her nose at the smell around the rabbit hutches, but rabbit stew would keep us alive.

I took my new business seriously. Every morning I slipped out to a nearby park to clip grass for their feed. They ate old cabbage leaves too, and whatever vegetables we could spare. I nearly lost everything when I fed them potato peelings. Potato peelings are not good for rabbits.

When the rabbits were big enough, Maman and I traded them for food, clothing, and even coal. What we didn't sell or trade, we ate. I was always careful to make sure to have at least two females and one male.

I felt I had done one more thing to make Papa proud. It was like I was building a ladder, rung by rung. How many rungs would I have to climb before I made up for what I'd done to Georges?

★ CHAPTER SIX ★

Pearl Harbor

December 1941

From the beginning, people spoke in whispers about America entering the war and beating the Germans. We all hoped for it, but not in the way that it happened. In December 1941, the Japanese bombed an American navy base. The United States declared war on Japan. Germany and Italy declared war on the United States. The whole world was at war.

Maman was immediately worried about her family who lived on Long Island in New York. The base at Pearl Harbor, Hawaii, was far from the United States mainland. Still, we knew that many of our cousins and uncles would find themselves in uniform like Papa and Georges.

German-controlled Radio Paris said that the entire American fleet was destroyed, and America was defeated. But then we heard parts of President Roosevelt's speech on the BBC. He vowed to fight, and to win.

The Germans congratulated each other as if they were the ones who had dropped the bombs. I wanted to drop a bomb on them, especially when they said the Americans had already been beaten.

One day I was walking past a German-only outdoor café with Jacques. The sun was shining and it was almost warm. A *boche* stood with a swastika flag draped around him and his arm up in the air. I didn't realize what he was doing until he spoke.

I only understood the words "Lady Liberty."

He was pretending to be the Statue of Liberty—France's gift to the United States. A symbol of freedom. The idea of the statue draped in the swastika made me want to rip the flag from his shoulders and strangle him with it. Instead I could only glare at him. I was as helpless as one of my rabbits. I blinked back tears of rage.

Jacques pulled me away. "There's nothing you

can do now," he said. "The Americans will come. Just wait."

I wiped tears from my cheeks, feeling weak and embarrassed. "This is it for the Nazis!" I told Jacques. "This is the beginning of the end. The Americans will defeat the Germans, even if they have to kill every last one of them. They never lose."

"The beginning of the end," Jacques agreed.

It was one of the rare conversations I had with Jacques that winter. He was always too busy to spend time with me. He made excuses instead of plans for resistance missions. Without Jacques, I lacked the courage to plan anything big. He was just as busy in the spring. One day in April I walked home from school alone—again—because Jacques had to run an errand for his mother.

I offered to go with him, as I had many times before. He said no.

"I have to rush to get there before they close, and you can't run fast in your *sabots*," he said.

That part was true. On my twelfth birthday in February, Maman and I had tried to find a new pair of shoes with my ration coupon. All we could find was a pair of wooden *sabots*. Nearly everyone wore them now—all the leather was sent to Germany—but they were clumsy and hard to run in. Even so, I knew that my shoes weren't the reason Jacques didn't want me with him. Was he afraid to be seen with me because I was half American?

We worried the Nazis would arrest Maman when the United States entered the war, but so far they continued to concentrate their hatred on the Jews. They blamed the Jews for everything that was wrong in France.

The Young Guards organized demonstrations and stood at the entrances of Jewish stores to scare business away. Stefan bragged about it in school and was rewarded with a treat by our teacher. One day the Guards went up and down the Champs-Élysées smashing the windows of Jewish-owned stores, breaking doors, and over-turning counters. The French police did nothing to stop them.

That same evening I saw Pierre on the *métro* train with Stefan and a group of Young Guards. My old friend was wearing the black shirt, along with a beret and the badge. Their voices could be heard from one end of the subway car to the other.

"Did you see the look on that old Jew's face?" Stefan asked with a laugh.

Another boy crooked his finger over his nose—

the anti-Jewish posters always showed them with big, hooked noses—and said in a shaky, old-man voice, "Boys! Boys! Stop that. I'll call the *gendarmes*."

"We are the police, Jew," Stefan said, putting a fist in the other boy's face. "And we'll do what we like."

"*Pow!*" Pierre yelled, punching the air.

They burst out laughing. The look of pride and excitement on my friend's face was unmistakable. I must have gasped because Pierre turned and his expression became one of cold stone. Then he nudged Stefan and whispered.

Stefan eyed me and spoke quietly to the entire group. They walked toward my end of the subway car and surrounded me in harsh silence. I pretended not to notice their clenched fists, but I could feel their eyes drilling into me like bullets. I focused on their feet. They all wore black leather boots.

I couldn't bear to sit there, but I didn't want them to see how frightened I was either. At the next stop I jumped to my feet and pushed past them with my head down. One of them tripped me in my clumsy wooden shoes and I heard them laughing as I stumbled through the doors. As the subway pulled out of the station, Pierre raised his arm in the Nazi salute and gave me a big smile. I sat down on a bench, stunned and scared. What had happened to my friend?

The Germans tried to make it seem that the anti-Jewish restrictions had come from the French and not the Germans, but I knew better. Still, more and more Frenchmen openly discriminated against the Jews. Eventually, Jewish businesses were placed under non-Jewish management. Then Jewish homes were taken from their owners and given to Nazis and their collaborators. Last month, only six months after the Japanese bombed Pearl Harbor, the Germans announced that all Jews over the age of six had to wear a yellow star, stamped with the word *juif.*

But even with all of the mistreatment and all of the rumors, I was not prepared for the French police to begin arresting Jews. But they were, right on my street and in my apartment building. Then, suddenly, Jacques was knocking on my kitchen window, holding Sophie Grossman's hand, and Maman had lied to the police. The little girl was hiding in my closet, and now I needed to know what to do next.

CHAPTER SEVEN

Good-bye, Sophie

July 16, 1942

As soon as the police left our street, I climbed the fire escape to Jacques's kitchen window. Jacques sat at the table with his sixteen-year-old brother, François. I gave the window a light tap and they both jumped. Jacques opened the window and I climbed in.

"*Ça va?*" Jacques asked.

"*Ça va,*" I answered. "All is well. Do you have Ernst?"

Jacques nodded.

François glared at me and then at his brother.

"You shouldn't have gotten him involved," he said to Jacques.

"I had no choice," Jacques told his brother. "You said to split them up." Then he turned to me. "Can you take Sophie to the train station?" he asked. "The *Gare d'Austerlitz*?"

I nodded, but I was confused. "She and Ernst can't take a train by themselves," I said.

"A nun will be on the platform, waiting for the three-fifteen train to Bordeaux," Jacques said. "She's bringing orphans to a convent in the country. Sophie and Ernst will be with them."

"Does it have to be today? What if the police are still around?" I asked.

"The nun leaves today," François said. "If we don't get Sophie and Ernst on that train, I don't know when—or if—we'll be able to get them out of Paris."

"What if there's more than one nun on the platform?" I asked. "What's her name?"

"No names," François snapped. "She'll be the nun surrounded by children."

I felt my cheeks redden. I had asked a stupid question. "You can trust me," I told him. "Do you want me to take Ernst too?"

"Jacques will bring Ernst. It's safer that way," François said. "If one of you gets picked up by the *boches,* the other will get away."

I was shocked that he could speak of one of us getting picked up in such a matter-of-fact way. Jacques rolled his eyes and smiled at me, as if to say, *Don't worry.*

"Jacques will leave first," François continued. "He'll knock on your door when he leaves. You'll follow ten minutes later. Take the *métro.*"

"Okay," I said.

"Get rid of her yellow star," François told me. "If anyone recognizes Sophie or calls her name, pretend you don't hear them. Keep your head down and keep going."

François's serious tone scared me, but I only nodded.

"Go now," he said. "Wait for Jacques's signal. Be ready."

I tried to ignore the fear that had begun to grip me and climbed out the window. I took one last look at Jacques before I set off down the stairs.

"*À bientôt,*" he said. "I'll wait for you at the station."

"See you later," I said. I tried to smile at him, but I could tell my expression was grim.

While Maman quickly packed food for Sophie, I went to my room to collect the little girl. I used a pair of scissors to snip the careful stitches holding the yellow star in place and plucked the loose threads.

"I am taking you to Ernst," I said, trying to sound cheerful. "And then a nice lady is going to bring you both to the country on a train. You'll be safe there until the Nazis let your parents go." No one knew what happened to the Jews they sent out of Paris, but I couldn't send Sophie away without saying something hopeful. "You have to be very brave until we get there. Can you do that?"

Sophie nodded. The corners of her mouth seemed to be turned down permanently.

"You're a big girl," I said. "I know you can."

We waited in the living room for Jacques's knock. Charlotte gave Sophie a rag doll made from one of Maman's old dresses, and Maman made sure that Sophie had enough food for at least three meals.

We all jumped when it came. Three quick taps and then a harder knock. I checked the clock— set to French time, not German—and waited exactly ten minutes.

After a hurried good-bye, I walked Sophie

quickly past the concierge, hoping that Madame Cassou wouldn't stop me and see that I had Sophie and not my sister, Charlotte, by the hand. The concierge took care of our apartment building and saw everything from her first-floor window. There was little that escaped her attention. Today I rushed by without a hello or a even a nod—an insult that could lead to "lost" pieces of mail and misplaced deliveries, if not a week's worth of gossip.

The street was quiet. There was nothing to indicate the uproar of this morning. On the next block, the police were still rounding up Jews. People like the Grossmans were being herded onto ordinary green-and-white buses. The kind of buses we saw every day. Children had their faces and hands plastered up against the windows as if they were on a field trip for school. What if Sophie's mother and father were on one of those buses? What if she saw them and called out to them, or someone called out to her?

I knelt and pretended to tie Sophie's shoe, whispering instructions. "Keep your head down," I said. "If someone calls your name, don't look. Don't answer. Pretend you don't hear. Keep walking."

She nodded and I stood to take her hand

again. She clutched Charlotte's doll in the other, while I carried her food package. I had to force myself not to run. The walk to the *métro* station seemed to take forever. I could feel Sophie's hand trembling in mine. She kept her head down, her eyes on her feet, but one tear and then another plopped onto her shoes.

I tried to steady myself with deep breaths, but when we passed a policeman my heart raced. He didn't look up from his clipboard. Was Sophie's name on one of his lists?

We rode the *métro* without anything unusual happening. It was crowded, but I nudged Sophie into an open seat and stood in front of her, blocking her from as many people as I could. There was still a chance that someone might recognize her.

At the *Gare d'Austerlitz* stop I breathed a sigh of relief and tried to sound cheerful. "You'll see your brother any minute," I told her as we climbed the stairs to the street. "He'll be happy to see you."

We rounded the corner and almost banged right into a German checkpoint.

★ CHAPTER EIGHT ★

Nazi Checkpoint

A Nazi checkpoint. I could feel myself beginning to panic, but I didn't want to alarm Sophie. Normally they only demanded the papers of the people arriving at the station, not those who were leaving the city. Did they know that Jewish children were slipping out of Paris, or was this just bad luck—one of those surprise inspections the Nazis used to keep us off balance?

Questions raced through my mind. Had Jacques and Ernst gotten past the checkpoint? I could go back home and hide Sophie until François could find another way to get her out of Paris, but then what would happen to Ernst? Would he and Sophie ever find each other again? I had to come up with a plan. I had my student identity card with me. Sophie's—if she even had hers—was stamped with the word *Jew*. There was no way we could hand it over.

The closer we got to the soldier the more my heart raced. Sophie's hand held mine with an iron grip. Could I pretend we had forgotten Sophie's card? I had to hope she would play along.

"Papers," the soldier demanded in a bored way.

I handed him my card. He looked at it, and then glanced at Sophie.

"Charlotte," I said. "Give the soldier your identity card."

Sophie kept her eyes trained on her shoes. Her whole body began to tremble.

"Don't tell me you forgot it," I said, in the sternest voice I could muster. "I told you to get it from Maman's purse. You're old enough to remember. Now we have to go back home. We'll be late to meet Auntie Colette's train."

Sophie crumpled into me and began to weep. I wanted to take her in my arms, but I continued to act the part of the irritated big brother. "Maman will be very angry with us, and it's all your fault."

It was only then that I noticed a single yellow thread sticking out of her lapel. It seemed as bright as the July sun against her gray coat. My mouth went dry. I waited for the Nazi to grab her arm and shout that she was a Jew. Instead, he seemed amused. He patted Sophie on the head. She flinched and let out a wail.

"Go ahead, little one," he said. "Don't keep your auntie waiting. But don't forget your papers next time."

"Merci," I muttered, and dragged Sophie past him. "Thank you."

As soon as we were out of his sight and in the busy train station, I pulled Sophie aside and tried to calm her. "I'm sorry I yelled at you," I said. "Don't worry. Everything will be fine."

Her sobs quieted to gentle sniffles. "Come," I whispered. "It's time to find Ernst."

We made our way to the platform for the three-fifteen train to Bordeaux with a few minutes to spare. Scared-looking children surrounded a nun. Sophie ran to Ernst with a cry. As soon I saw that the nun had registered Sophie's presence, I handed Sophie her food parcel and edged away. Three more children arrived, all carrying bundles.

I waited at the back of the platform. The train

arrived belching black smoke. Passengers got off and the nun herded the children and their small parcels into a compartment. Sophie and Ernst clung to each other. Suddenly I was terribly sad to see them go. I almost felt as if I was putting Charlotte on a train, not knowing who would take care of her or if I would ever see her again. Sophie and Ernst looked so small, and so unable to defend themselves.

I waited until the train pulled out. Only then did I see Jacques at the other end of the platform. He was leaning against the wall with a newspaper tucked under his arm. He nodded slightly and slipped into the busy station. I kept my eyes trained on my friend and rushed to catch up. A businessman banged into him, and Jacques handed the man his newspaper. Then he vanished into the crowd while the businessman rushed in the other direction. One minute Jacques was there and the next he was gone. When did he learn to do that?

Now I knew what Jacques was doing all those afternoons he couldn't walk home with me, all those times I had asked him to plan resistance missions. Jacques had become a soldier—a real solider for France. While I had been playing at being a *résistant* like a child, scrawling *V*s on walls and giving the *boches* wrong directions, Jacques had taken on the work of a man.

I walked across the station to an exit on the opposite side of the building so that the same *boche* wouldn't ask what had become of my sister and my aunt. I found myself imagining a conversation with Papa after the war. He would tell us about the work he did for General de Gaulle in London, and Georges would describe the terrible things the Nazis did to him before he led his fellow prisoners in a daring escape and blew up a Nazi munitions factory.

Then Papa would turn to me. "And what did you do, little one, besides hand your brother over to the enemy?"

He would laugh at my resistance efforts and my small black-market business. "Children's games," he would scoff. "You played games and nursed bunnies while your brother was forced to slave for the Nazis."

I wanted him to be proud of me. I wanted him to believe that I had done something important. Now I realized that I would have to do more.

Jacques waited for me at the entrance to the *métro*. We got on the subway and rode home together as if nothing had happened. I had a million questions, but couldn't ask until there was no chance that we would be overheard.

Finally we reached our stop and were back on the street. "Why didn't you tell me?" I asked. "Why didn't you ask for my help?"

"François wouldn't let me," Jacques explained quietly.

"I understand," I said, although that was a lie. Didn't Jacques know he could trust me with anything? But now wasn't the time for hurt feelings. Now was the time for action. "I want to join the real Resistance. Tell me how."

"It's dangerous," he warned.

"I know. I'm still in."

"I'll tell François," he said. "We need you."

I shook his hand solemnly. "The flame of resistance," I said.

"Must not be extinguished," he answered.

I headed to my apartment knowing that there was no turning back. From now on I would lead a double life. In one, I would continue to be a good son and student, a child. In the other, I would be a soldier, striking out at the Nazis in any way possible.

★ CHAPTER NINE ★

The Wolf

September 1942

I waited weeks for Jacques to give me a secret job. Finally, one day after school, he asked me to join him upstairs. Everyone in the Dubois family was out except for him and François.

The three of us sat at the kitchen table. François laid out the rules. Rule number one was never use your real name, or refer to other people by theirs.

"It's unfortunate that you know us and we know you," François said. "You must remember to call Jacques by his real name in your everyday life, and by his *nom de guerre* when you are working."

"My war name is Fox," Jacques said.

François nodded. "I am Lion."

Lion? I almost snorted about the idea of François as king of the jungle, but he and Jacques were so serious that I bit my tongue.

I would have to choose a secret name myself. My first thought was Rabbit, because I had to go home and feed mine, but I did not want to be a gentle creature. I wanted to be fierce. "I will be Wolf," I told them.

I waited for them to laugh, but Jacques nodded seriously.

"Wolf," François repeated. "Don't tell anyone your real name or anything about yourself. It's safer that way," he explained. "If you get picked up by the Gestapo, you won't be able to do too much damage to the rest of the operation."

I drew myself up. "I would never tell resistance secrets to the Gestapo," I insisted.

"They torture people for information," François said flatly. "They threaten your family. Many people older and stronger than you have cracked under the pressure."

Jacques nodded solemnly.

Torture? I thought about putting an end to the whole adventure, but then I thought about Papa and what I would tell him after the war and about how brave my teacher had been in speaking out against the new motto. I shook off my fear. "What will I have to do?" I asked.

"You'll know when the time comes," François snapped. "Follow orders. Don't ask questions. You're a soldier in a secret war. A dangerous war. The smallest mistake could lead to many arrests."

I felt like I had been slapped. "Fine," I snapped back. "Let me know when the time comes."

Jacques followed me to the door and gave me a sarcastic smile. "Don't mind the Lion," he said, rolling his eyes.

"It's just that if I'm going to risk my life, I should at least know what I'm going to do," I said.

"I don't think he knows," Jacques said. "He gets instructions from one person and passes them on. We do what's necessary," he told me. "The less we know, the better, but the work is important."

"What do your parents think you're doing?" I asked.

"François announced one night at dinner that he was joining the Resistance and it was best if they never asked him any questions. They tried to talk him out of it, but he refused to change his mind. What could they do?" Jacques asked. "Turn him in to the *Kommandantur*?"

"What about you?" I asked.

"I talked François into letting me help. It's easier for boys to move around the city than grownups," Jacques said.

Maman had figured out that Jacques and I wrote on Nazi posters and posted victory stickers in the subway, but I didn't think she'd let me do the kind of work Jacques and his brother did.

"Does your *maman* know?" I asked.

"She spends so many afternoons on line at the shops that I'm not sure she does," Jacques said. "I'm never out at night, only after school."

I nodded. It was possible that Maman would never find out that my resistance activities had changed. Like Mrs. Dubois, she spent a good part of her day lining up in front of shops, hoping to buy food, or trading rabbits on the black market. If she didn't know, then I wouldn't be putting her or Charlotte in any danger. Besides, I told myself, the real danger was in letting the Germans win.

A few days went by with no word from the Lion. I worried that he had changed his mind. Then, one afternoon after school, Jacques asked me to join him for a bike ride. Finally, I thought, real resistance work!

"It's best not to take the *métro* if you can avoid it," Jacques explained later. "Too many German patrols."

We bicycled to a street near the Bastille and stopped in front of an apartment building. Jacques, or the Fox, casually looked up at a window on the fourth floor. "Remember this address," he said. "Never write it down."

I closed my eyes and committed the address to memory.

"If there is a mop hanging from the third window from the left, we must not go up," Jacques said. "Don't make it obvious that you're looking."

I tried to look without looking. There was no mop.

The building's concierge eyed us with a bored expression. Jacques waved to her as we parked our bikes in the courtyard. I followed him up the stairs to the fourth floor.

Jacques gave the door three light taps. A woman answered and drew us inside with a smile.

"This is Wolf," Jacques told her. "He'll come in my place sometimes."

"I'm Bluebird," she said.

She looked like a bluebird. Small and cheerful and happy with big, blue eyes. She offered us a snack, which Jacques refused. I also shook my head no. I was almost always hungry, but today my stomach churned with anxiety. I still had no idea what dangerous mission Jacques and I would carry out.

Bluebird handed me a sealed envelope. Jacques told me to slip it inside my jacket. I tucked it under my arm. Then we set off again.

I knew not to ask questions, but I wondered what was in the envelope. It was thin. Was it money to bribe *boches*? False identity cards? Blueprints of Nazi headquarters that the Resistance wanted to bomb? I kept my arm clamped tight to my side to make sure I wouldn't lose whatever I carried.

Jacques kept up a casual conversation about school while we rode our bikes to a café in the eighth *arrondissement*. We had to cross the busy Champs-Élysées. I stiffened every time I saw a Nazi soldier, but Jacques was completely relaxed.

"Don't worry," he told me. "You'll get used to it."

We stopped on a corner near a sidewalk café. Jacques pointed out a woman with the slightest nod of his head. She sat at a table reading a book and sipping a cup of tea. One glove had dropped to the sidewalk by her foot. Jacques took the envelope from me and rode his bike toward her. When he got close, he stopped short and bent down to pick up the glove.

"Your glove, *madame*," he said. He handed it to her along with the envelope.

The woman's face betrayed nothing. She accepted the glove and the envelope with a bored expression. "*Merci,* young man," she said.

"My friend and I wouldn't want you to lose it."

Only then did her eyes flick to me and then away. "Thank you," she said again.

Jacques and I bicycled away. Our work was done for the day.

I looked at my friend with a new admiration. He had carried out his job so smoothly that only those watching very carefully would have noticed the exchange. Would I be able to do it as well?

★ CHAPTER TEN ★

"Are You Looking
for Me?"

A few days later, Jacques and I picked up another envelope from the Bluebird and took it
to same café on the Champs-Élysées. This time a
tall man sat reading. He must have taken off his
beret and set it on the table, only to have it fall to
the ground. Jacques explained that sometimes the
man and sometimes the woman waited for the envelope. He did not know their names—not even
their code names. If the glove or the hat was not
on the ground, I was to ride on.

This time I was the one who rode toward the
man and stopped short to give him his hat along

with the envelope. My hand trembled and my voice was much too loud when I said, "Your hat, *monsieur.*"

The man's eyes flicked from me to Jacques and back to me again.

"Thank you, young man," he said with a nod.

After that, I ran the errand myself. No one ever told me what was in the envelopes, but once or twice a week Jacques would whisper to me that the Bluebird expected a visit. The person in the café never said more than thank you. Everything went smoothly, and I even grew a little bored with my assignment. My childish version of resistance work was a lot more fun than this new job.

Then one day in November there was a strange man at the table. No one told me to expect a new contact, but the man's beret sat at his feet, as it should. Still, something wasn't right. He made idle chitchat with the man at the next table instead of reading like the others had done.

I rode past him and made a loop around the block. This time I stopped at the corner and studied this new person. I watched him call out to a pretty girl who walked by. His French was perfect. He didn't sound German.

Suddenly I realized why I was troubled. The man was too loud, and too well fed. Only the Germans had enough to eat, and a good *résistant* would never draw attention to himself in public. Even I knew that.

The man chuckled at the way the girl ignored him and then sat back with a sigh. He took out a package of cigarettes.

I froze.

The package was a German brand.

I felt as if I was being lit on fire when he brought a match to the tip of his cigarette and drew the smoke into his lungs. The man was a Nazi, or one of their collaborators, and whatever I carried in my envelope was definitely *verboten*.

His eyes swept the street and came to rest on my bicycle and me. He smiled.

"Young man, are you looking for me?"

A *résistant* would never ask such a question in a public place for others to hear.

He tapped his foot next to his beret, trying to draw my attention to it. I didn't want to look, but my eyes darted to his feet of their own accord. I could feel my face turning red, giving me away.

"Non, non, monsieur," I stammered. "I'm looking

for my maman. She must have already gone home. I'll . . . I'll go there now."

His face hardened and he eyed me suspiciously. I pretended not to notice. I wheeled my bike around and got ready to cross the busy Champs-Élysées. Out of the corner of my eye I saw him get to his feet.

"Wait," he yelled. "Wait."

I pretended not to hear him. I looked for a break in the traffic.

"Stop that boy," the man yelled in his perfect French. Then he switched to German. The only word I understood was *"Halt!"*

I heard footsteps behind me, and a loud whistle. A black Mercedes roared to life.

Gestapo!

My whole body flinched, but I pedaled into the traffic. I couldn't even throw the envelope away without being seen. I dodged German trucks, bicyclists, bicycle taxis, and pedestrians to reach the other side of the avenue. The Mercedes ignored every traffic law to stay on my tail. A truck barreled toward me. If I kept going, it would surely hit me. If I stopped, the Gestapo would get me.

Bang!

Bang!

Was that a gun? Fear gave me the push I needed. I pedaled furiously in front of the truck. It missed hitting me by the narrowest of slivers. The Mercedes was not so lucky. It crashed right into the truck.

I didn't look back. I rode all over Paris at top speed, hardly even daring to look over my shoulder to see if I was being followed. About an hour later I heard another loud bang. I flinched and almost crashed into a wall. It was a truck backfiring. That's when I realized—the *boches* hadn't shot at me on the Champs-Élysées. A truck had backfired.

That was a small relief, but I was worried about the envelope. Getting caught with it would mean death. I crossed the Seine half a dozen times. Each time I decided to throw the envelope into the river, and each time I changed my mind. No one had told me what to do if I couldn't carry out my mission. What if whatever was in that envelope would save the life of a soldier for France?

Finally, after riding for what felt like hours and making doubly and triply sure I wasn't being followed, I took the envelope home. It was dark by that time, and I knew Maman would be worried, but I rode the elevator to Jacques's floor instead of my own.

I knocked and collapsed to the floor outside his door, exhausted and trembling. Jacques found me there a few seconds later.

"Gestapo," I whispered.

★ CHAPTER ELEVEN ★

Arrests!

November 1942

Jacques helped me inside and brought me into the bedroom he shared with François. Now that my race through the streets was over, I was even more scared than I'd been when the Gestapo was on my heels. Jacques brought me a cup of tea and reached under his mattress for a chocolate bar—an American chocolate bar!

"Where?" I asked. I hadn't seen real chocolate since shortly after the war began.

"I'll tell you later," Jacques said. "What happened?"

I took a deep sniff of the chocolate and slipped

a piece into my mouth, letting it melt. I had forgotten that something could taste so good. Then I told Jacques everything from the moment I began to suspect my contact was a Nazi to my arrival at his door.

"Are you sure you weren't followed?" he asked.

"I made the Gestapo crash into a truck," I said. "I rode through every alley in Paris—most of them too narrow for cars. There's no way a man could run as fast as I pedaled." My leg muscles were still twitching.

Jacques nodded thoughtfully. "I was supposed to meet someone at the train station," he said. "He never arrived. I wonder if—" He shook himself. "We don't know anything yet, let's not panic."

"Not panic?" I asked. "I was almost caught by the Gestapo with this." I pointed to the envelope, which sat on the bed between us. My arm had been pressed so tightly to my side that there was a red welt on my skin from the edge of the envelope, and it was stained with my sweat.

"Do you know what's inside?" I asked.

Jacques shook his head. "I have an idea, but François never told me."

"If I'm going to be tortured by the Gestapo, I want to know what for," I said.

Jacques didn't argue. I opened the seal and spilled the envelope's contents onto the bed. Two faces looked back at me. There were identity cards for two men along with everything else they would need if they were stopped at a checkpoint: ration cards and coupons, work permits, travel permits, and medical release papers from the French army.

"Identity papers," I said.

Jacques nodded. "Forgeries. That's what I thought."

"Who are they for?" I asked.

Jacques leaned forward and whispered. "Aviators," he said. "British. American. Their airplanes were shot down over Belgium and France. We help them get to Spain so they can go back to England and fight again."

I gasped. "Americans!"

Jacques nodded. "We're part of an escape line that stretches all the way across France—like the American Underground Railroad for the slaves."

"Why didn't you tell me?" I asked.

Jacques struggled to come up with a reason. Finally he told the truth. "You're half American. Your *maman* is American. The Gestapo could arrest you at any time."

I felt as if I had been kicked in the stomach. The Resistance didn't trust me because I was American? It made no sense.

Jacques was about to tell me more, but we heard noise at the front door. We swept the papers back into the envelope and Jacques shoved it under his pillow.

François clattered into the bedroom. When he saw us, he leaned back against the door and slid to the floor. His hair stood up in a crazy-looking way and his eyes were wild.

"You're safe," he said, when his breathing had slowed enough for him to talk. "You're both safe." He closed his eyes and rested his head in his hands. His shoulders shook.

Panic shot through me again. François was crying.

Jacques and I pretended not to notice. By the time the Lion looked up at us again, he had gotten control of himself.

"My friend never arrived at the train station," Jacques said.

"The man at the café was German," I said, "or a collaborator. The Gestapo almost got me."

"Did they get the envelope?"

"No. I saw he wasn't right," I said.

Jacques pulled the envelope from under his pillow. François grabbed it and slid it under his shirt. He dragged his fingers through his black hair, making it stand up even more. "Bluebird was arrested," he said in a shaky voice. "Along with Giraffe. Others too."

Bluebird—everything was fine when I stopped at her apartment this afternoon. The Gestapo must have captured her right after I left.

François got to his feet and began to pace. "Have either of you ever shared your real name with anyone on the line?"

Jacques and I both shook our heads.

"We may be all right. We can only wait and see," he said. "Could the German recognize you if he saw you again?"

"Maybe," I admitted. "He saw me watching him and he tried to get me to make the exchange. I pretended not to understand, but he didn't believe me. I had to race away. The *boches* chased me, but I was too fast."

Jacques turned to François with a proud grin. "Wolf made the Gestapo drive his car right into a truck."

I pictured the accident and I began to laugh in a kind of hysterical way. It wasn't funny, really, but

I laughed so hard that tears ran down my face. Then I thought about Bluebird and the cheerful way she greeted me and offered me a snack every time I saw her, and the tears became real. Was the Gestapo torturing her right now?

I hid my face in Jacques's pillow and wept for her. Once the real tears started, I couldn't stop. I wept for Papa and Georges. I wept for France. And I wept for America.

Normally my tears would have been embarrassing, but even François had cried today. Jacques rubbed my shoulders the way Maman would have. When I was able to stop crying and sit up, I saw tears on his face too. We all cried for our comrades and our country.

"Do you know what happened?" I asked François.

He shook his head. "Someone gave us away—a collaborator or a Nazi. He wormed his way into the line, learned our secrets, and gave us up to the Gestapo."

"Has anyone else been arrested?" Jacques asked.

François shrugged. "I only know a few people in the chain, and I don't know any of their real names. The line stretches from Belgium to Spain. Many, many people help the aviators along the way." He started to pace again, making plans with each step. "We'll have to lie low for a while. Wait and see if the Resistance can rebuild the escape line."

"What about our friends who are already in Paris?" Jacques asked.

My eyes went wide. Jacques and François had aviators hidden in Paris?

"They'll have to stay here for a while," François said simply. He rubbed his belly and I heard the crinkle of paper under his shirt. "At least they have papers," he said. "If only they spoke French."

He took the envelope and left the room. I could hear a muffled argument between him and his parents. No one shouted, afraid the neighbors would hear, so I couldn't make out the words. Mr. and Mrs. Dubois sounded scared, but Francois's tone was determined. After a few minutes a door slammed, and the Lion went out into the night.

I had my own argument with Maman when I got home. She was worried. It was late, and the concierge had told her that I rushed into the building looking like I was being chased. She wanted me to tell her what I was doing, and where I had been—secrets I couldn't share with her—not safely. She wanted my promise that I would stop, but I couldn't do that either.

"Papa would want me to do this," I said. "I'm doing this for France. For Georges. And for Papa."

"Papa would want you to be safe," she said.

"Papa would want *Georges* to be safe," I said. Even I could hear the bitterness in my voice.

Surprise crossed her face. Did she really think I'd never noticed?

"Besides, I'm not in any real danger."

She stared at me for a long moment. She knew I was lying.

"I'm not," I said, my voice thick with tears.

She threw her hands up into the air. "Go to bed," she said. "But this isn't over. We're going to talk about this again."

I was too exhausted to argue. Too exhausted to listen for the Gestapo to knock on my or Jacques's door. But they didn't. Things were quiet for the next few days, and I thought we were safe. Then, the next week, the Nazis began to arrest Americans.

★ CHAPTER TWELVE ★

84 Avenue Foch

One afternoon when Jacques and I got home from school, Madame Cassou signaled to me from her window. "Gestapo," she whispered. "With your *maman*."

My whole body went cold. Were they here because Maman was American, or had someone identified me as the boy from the cafe?

"Did they go to my apartment too?" Jacques asked.

"No," Madame Cassou answered. Then she turned to me. "They want to know where your *papa* is."

"Papa is a prisoner," I said. Maman and I had stuck to that story since the day the Nazis marched into Paris. That's what we told everyone.

The concierge shrugged. "That's what I told them. You think they listen to me?"

The elevator wasn't working, so Jacques and I trudged up the stairs. My heavy *sabots* clunked against each step. Fear made me suspicious. I wondered if Jacques had turned us in to the *Kommandantur* to keep the Nazis from looking too closely at him and François. Then I shook off that crazy idea. My friend was no traitor.

I nodded good-bye to Jacques and opened the front door. There was no yelling, only quiet voices.

Maman was sitting on the couch, smoothing her skirt. Charlotte leaned into her. Two Gestapo agents sat across from them, one of them in Papa's favorite chair.

"Michel," Maman said.

She used the French pronunciation of my name instead of the more American "Michael." She hardly ever did that. She continued speaking French even though we often spoke to each other in English. Maman wanted us to be fluent in both languages.

I followed her lead. "Is something wrong, Maman?" I asked in French. "Has something happened to Papa or Georges?"

"No, don't worry," she said. "They're still in Germany. These officers need to ask me a few questions at their headquarters. I want you to come with us and look after Charlotte."

I nodded. Maman sounded so calm, so unworried. I was afraid to speak and betray my fear. My heart fluttered like a bird trying to get out of its cage. If the Gestapo just wanted to question Maman, I could look after Charlotte here at the apartment. They wanted all three of us at headquarters.

"Do I need to pack a bag?" Maman asked in French.

Even though Maman had asked him the question in French, the Nazi answered in heavily accented English. "Not necessary," he said. His eyes surveyed the room. Was he taking inventory, deciding which of our pieces of furniture he would keep when he took over our apartment?

Within minutes we were in the back of their black Mercedes. Maman gave my hand a squeeze and told me not to worry. We pulled up in front of 84 Avenue Foch, Gestapo headquarters. A soldier rushed to open the car doors, and we were led inside the most feared address in Paris.

Maman and I had had many discussions about what to do if the Nazis questioned us about Papa. We told Charlotte the same thing that we planned to tell the Nazis—Papa had disappeared in the Battle of France. We never mentioned, even to each other, that he was with General de Gaulle in England.

The Gestapo split the three of us up. Maman was led into an office with one of the Nazis. She wanted to bring Charlotte with her, but a German woman came and took my sister by the hand. Charlotte wailed, reaching for Maman and then for me. The other *boche* pulled me away.

"No one will harm her," he said in English.

I followed Maman's example and answered in French. "She's only five," I said. "And scared of soldiers. Yelling frightens her."

The *boche* snorted. "Who will yell at her?" he asked in English.

He led me into an office with two desks, an extra chair in the middle of the room, and a barred window. I could see more barred windows across a courtyard. The *boche* nudged me to the chair. I sat and took my coat off. It was warm. I hadn't been this warm in winter since before the war.

Obviously there was no shortage of coal for the Nazis, only for the French.

The officer exchanged a few sentences in German with a young soldier who sat at one of the desks. Then he switched to French, clearly for my benefit.

"The boy and his mother understand that we just want information," he said to the soldier. "They know it's best to cooperate." Then he turned to me and switched once again to his heavily accented English.

"Tell me about your father's activities in England," he said.

★ CHAPTER THIRTEEN ★

Questioned by the Gestapo

My jaw dropped. *"Quoi?"* I stammered. "What?"

"Tell me about your father's activities in England," the Gestapo agent said again, louder this time.

"What? What are you talking about?" I asked. "My *papa* isn't in England." Somehow I managed to remember to answer in French and not in English. It was important that he think of me as French, not American. The United States was at war with Germany. France had signed an armistice.

The *boche* switched topics as quickly and easily as he did languages. "You are American. Correct?"

"*Non.*" I shook my head. Once again, I answered him in French. "I am French. I was born in France," I told him. "Maman was born in the United States, but she is a French citizen—for twenty years."

His mouth tightened into a grim line. "Why do you refuse to speak English? You understand it."

"I understand English better than I speak it," I said in French. I said the next sentence in English, but exaggerated my French accent and made sure to get the grammar wrong. "Not good is my English."

He gave up. The next question was in French. "You have spent much time in America?"

"Before the war," I said vaguely. "A holiday or two with Maman's family."

"And your father? How does he feel about America?"

"America?" I asked. That question genuinely surprised me. I shrugged. "Papa's a Frenchman. His loyalties are to France."

"Where is your *papa* now?" he asked.

I stared at him for a moment. Hadn't he just said Papa was in England? "We don't know. We think he was at Dunkirk. Maman believes he is a prisoner. But we've heard nothing. I'm afraid he's dead."

The Nazi said nothing. I continued to babble. "My brother, Georges, is a prisoner. We got a post-card from him. He's working in Germany."

The Gestapo agent dropped the topic of England completely. Did he know that Papa was in England, or was he just fishing? He asked many questions about America. He acted as if we were having a pleasant conversation in a café or something. I remembered Pierre's ugly words about Americans, and I repeated them now, as if they were my beliefs. The words tasted bitter in my mouth, but the *boche* agreed enthusiastically.

"Yes! Yes! Americans are all about money."

He asked about our contact with our American relatives. There was none that I knew of. The war had put a stop to that.

The Gestapo stepped into the hall. I asked the younger solider for some water. I knew he understood French, but he ignored me. When the Gestapo returned, he was angry. "Your father is in England." he screamed. "Plotting against the Third Reich, and you are helping him." His face was red. Spittle flew from his lips. "Tell me everything and it will be better for you—and your *maman*."

That last part sounded like a threat, but I had nothing to tell. I said nothing.

The *boche* slammed his fist down on the desk and I jumped.

"He is spying for the Americans. You and your mother are helping him gather information."

My jaw dropped. His statement was so ridiculous that I would have burst out laughing had I not been so frightened. "What information?" I asked. "We have no information. We know nothing."

"Where is your father?" the *boche* asked again.

"I don't know," I answered. "Dead or in Germany."

The *boche* took a deep breath. "Your mother has told us. I only want you to confirm a few details, and then you can all go home. I can't help you if you don't want to help yourself. If you don't want to help your *maman*." He threw his arms up in the air and waited.

I said nothing.

"Your sister is alone," he said. "She is scared."

My mind raced. I didn't believe Maman had strayed from our story. It was possible that Papa was living openly in England, working for de Gaulle. The Gestapo would know that. But Maman and I had no contact with him. How could we? Where had the Germans gotten this ridiculous idea that Maman and I were spies for Papa?

If the Gestapo had any real facts, the officer wouldn't keep asking the same questions over and over again, trying to trip me up. I could trust Maman. She could trust me. My fear left me and I was filled with an icy calm.

"I do want to help Maman," I said, "but I have nothing to tell you. We have not heard from Papa since before the Occupation."

Sometimes the *boche* was conversational and friendly. Other times he screamed and pounded his desk. I answered the questions the same way over and over and over again. All the while the young soldier sat calmly taking notes.

Then it occurred to me that a little playacting might help.

"Do you know where my *papa* is?" I asked. "Is he really alive in England?"

The Nazi refused to answer.

I was tired and hungry, and suddenly a wave of sadness washed over me. I had said over and over again that I feared Papa was dead. What if he really was? What if he would never know how much I tried to be a soldier for France? I dropped my head into my hands and began to cry.

"Stop that," the *boche* said.

"My *papa* is dead, isn't he?" I wailed. "You worked him to death in Germany!"

The *boche* slammed out of the room.

I sat there for a long time, wondering what had sent the Gestapo to our home in the first place.

"Please," I begged the silent young soldier. "Do you know anything about my *papa*?"

He didn't answer.

I wondered why the Nazis hadn't asked me any questions about the Resistance. Had someone turned Maman in as an American and made up lies about us for a few extra pieces of coal?

An hour later, the *boche* came back and flicked his hand in dismissal. The younger man stood, clicked his heels, and with a *"Heil Hitler"* led me into the hall. They were the only words I heard him speak.

Charlotte sat on a bench with the German lady. She ran to me and threw her arms around my waist.

"Où est Maman?" she asked. "Where is Maman?"

"She'll be here soon," I said. I led Charlotte

back to the bench and we sat, hugging, under the watchful gaze of the German lady. Finally an agent led a tired, scared, but very determined-looking Maman to us.

Charlotte threw herself at Maman.

"Shhhh, *ma petite.*" Maman gathered Charlotte in her arms. "All is well, my darling. All is well." She looked over Charlotte's head to where I sat. I was suddenly too tired to even stand. *"Ça va?"* she asked.

"Ça va, Maman," I answered. "All is well."

With Charlotte between us, we walked out the front doors of Gestapo headquarters and splurged on a bicycle taxi.

"Papa would be very proud of you," Maman said, once we were far away from Avenue Foch.

"He would be proud of *you,*" I told her. Secretly, I couldn't help worrying that I had done something to bring the Gestapo to our door. Did they suspect my resistance work?

The Gestapo left us alone after that. Maman had to register at the local police station every Saturday to prove she was still in Paris. We weren't allowed to leave the city.

"That's all right," Maman said, hugging Charlotte. "We like Paris. We'll be here when the Americans and the English come and drive these nasty *boches* back to Germany."

Charlotte looked up at her with a sleepy smile. "Nasty *boches*," she repeated.

★ CHAPTER FOURTEEN ★

A Traitor Revealed

Maman believed that the Gestapo had questioned us only because she was American, but I wasn't so sure. How did they know that Papa was in England? Maman had told no one. I told my two closest friends, and one of them had turned into a Nazi. I suspected Pierre.

I knew for sure when I arrived at the schoolyard with Jacques two days later. Pierre nearly tripped over his feet in surprise. He tried to act unconcerned, but I saw it—shock, fear, and disbelief crossed his face. Pierre did not expect to see me at school that day, or ever again.

"He did it," I said to Jacques.

Jacques nodded. He'd seen it too.

I raised my fists, ready to pound the traitor into the pavement. I saw fear in my ex-friend's eyes. He searched the schoolyard, no doubt looking for his accomplice. Stefan was nowhere in sight. Pierre was only brave when the Young Guards surrounded him.

Now he slithered into the school building.

I set off after him, but Jacques caught up and held me back. "You'll only get into trouble," he said. "You don't want him going to the Nazis again, do you?"

"Maybe I'll go to the *Kommandantur* and turn him in on a made-up charge," I said from between clenched teeth. "He can learn what it's like to be interrogated by the Gestapo."

"No *Kommandantur*," Jacques said. "The Resistance will deal with him and the other Nazi collaborators after the war. François says the *collabos* will be tried for their war crimes as soon as we drive the Nazis out of France."

Jacques was right, of course. But at that moment I wanted nothing more than to see Pierre suffer. To see him bleed. I took deep breaths until I was able to unclench my fists. I had calmed down, but my vow to fight the Nazis was stronger than ever.

"When do I start helping the aviators again?" I asked. "The sooner they get back to England, the sooner they can win this war. And then—I promise you—I will take care of Pierre myself."

"Soon," Jacques said. "Soon."

It wouldn't be soon enough for me. Christmas was just a month away, and December meant it would be even colder. We French shivered in our patched clothing, went without Christmas presents, and faced near-empty dinner tables. German soldiers carried packages wrapped in colorful paper and planned elaborate Christmas feasts.

As 1942 drew to a close, things in France began to change. The Allies landed in North Africa and liberated the French colonies. We began to truly believe that Germany would lose the war. I guess the Nazis were beginning to believe that too. Until then, they occupied only the Atlantic coast and the northern part of France. But when they lost North Africa, the Nazis rushed to take over the rest of the country. They also started going after the Resistance with a fierceness we had not seen before.

In January, Jacques began to disappear on mysterious errands again. That meant the Resistance had been able to rebuild the escape line. François refused to send me out on missions. He thought the Gestapo might be watching because I was American.

I spent the next three weeks breaking the rules just to prove him wrong. I tore down more posters, pinned a paper *V* on my jacket, and even stuck a *Vive de Gaulle* sticker right on the back of a German truck. The real test came when I found a pile of resistance newsletters on the *métro* and spent the afternoon slipping them into people's hands. I even handed one to a Nazi soldier just as the subway doors were closing. By the time he realized what he was reading, I had jumped onto the platform. As the train pulled out of the station, the Nazi shook his fist at me, but I escaped without arrest. If the Gestapo was watching, I'd have been dragged off to headquarters five or six times.

Finally, François had to admit that the Resistance needed me. The Nazis were arresting French men and forcing them to go to Germany to work in war factories. They raided cafés and movie houses, the *métro*, and every other public place. No one over eighteen was safe. Men had to go underground, and the Resistance needed boys, despite the risks.

One Saturday morning in March, right after I got back from clipping grass for my rabbits, Jacques asked me if I had any English books.

"A few, I said. "Maman has more."

"Can you come with me?" he asked. "And bring a couple of books?"

Jacques had told me weeks ago that he and François were helping American and British aviators. If he wanted English books, that could only mean I was going to meet one of them! I slipped copies of *Huckleberry Finn* and *Treasure Island* into my rucksack and followed Jacques on a bike ride across town. We stopped in front of a small house in the Pigalle neighborhood. I stood back while the Fox quietly knocked on a door. An old woman led us into a cramped kitchen.

"*Bonjour, madame,*" Jacques said. "This is the friend I told you about. The Wolf."

The old woman smiled and kissed my cheeks.

"*Bonjour,*" I said. I was disappointed. What could this old woman possibly have to do with the Resistance?

"Come," she said. She led us into a small, dark living room. The curtains were pinned closed. A man was sleeping on a sofa. One leg dangled over the armrest. The other was propped on cushions. He was way too big for the furniture.

The old woman cleared her throat and the man woke with a start. He tried to get to his feet, but only teetered on his good leg. His eyes darted from me to Jacques to the old woman. *"Ami?"* the man asked Jacques in badly accented French. "Friend?"

"Friend and comrade," I assured him in English. "You must be American!"

★ CHAPTER FIFTEEN ★

An American Aviator

March 1943

The aviator stared at me with a stunned expression. He looked familiar. I thought about it for a few minutes and then I realized that his was one of the faces on the identity cards Jacques and I had looked at on the day of the arrests.

Jacques laughed at the man's surprise and explained what had happened. "He's been here since the arrests. The line was finally up and running again when he tripped in the dark and sprained his ankle—badly. He's lucky he didn't break it, but he can't leave until he can walk. He's been trapped in this small dark room ever since."

The American looked to me, and I translated. "Jacques says you're stuck here until your ankle heals," I said.

"I didn't tell him you were coming," Jacques continued. "I didn't want to get his hopes up if the Lion said no, but he's starting to act a little strange. I think he's been without anyone to talk to for too long."

The old woman pointed to her chest. "I don't speak English," she said in French.

The pilot understood that at least. "I don't speak French," he added. "I haven't heard my own language for weeks. They don't even have a radio here."

"The Germans block the BBC anyway," I told him. "They don't want us to know they're losing the war. Where are you from?"

"Lexington, Kentucky. Name is Steve Jones."

He was a giant of a man, much taller than the average Frenchman. I wondered where the Resistance had found clothes to fit him, but then I noticed that someone had sewn fabric onto the ends of his trouser legs so that they would cover his ankles. His shirt was at least two sizes too small.

"I'm Wolf," I said.

He gave my hand a hard shake. "Hiya, Wolfie,"

the pilot said. "It sure is nice to hear English. And you don't even have an accent. Where'd y'all learn it?"

"My mother—" I cut myself off again. If the Nazis picked up Steve Jones from Lexington, Kentucky, he could lead them to me. Or worse, to Maman.

"Is your mother an American?" he asked.

"No, but she speaks the language very well," I said. It surprised me how easily and naturally I lied. Keeping secrets had become second nature. "I learned it from her."

I visited Steve every few days for the next couple of weeks. Sometimes I rode my bike, sometimes the *métro*. I took different routes, and went at different times of day, always watching to make sure I wasn't being followed. The aviator devoured every book I brought him and was anxious for every bit of war news I had. The Germans had done a good job of blocking the radio waves, but every once in a while some good news got through to us.

Steve couldn't tell me what I really wanted to know—when the Allies would invade France and drive the *boches* out—but he told me his own story.

"I was a gunner on a B-17," he said, "a Flying

Fortress. It was our fifth mission. We were flying over France, toward Germany, to take out a factory just over the French-German border. We were close to our target when the Luftwaffe showed up on our tail. Planes around us started going down. Next thing I knew, there was a loud *whump,* and my buddy Pete crumpled to the floor. Dead."

Steve stared into space for a minute. "I crippled one of their planes," he said, "but they kept coming at us. Our plane started to nose-dive—fast. The copilot screamed over the radio that we had to bail. The next thing I knew, I was jumping out of the plane. Only a couple of us got out before the engine exploded."

I wanted to hear more, but he'd stopped talking. The horror on his face kept me from asking what happened next. Steve took a few minutes to collect himself and then told the rest of the story. He had dangled in the air while his parachute slowly drifted to the ground. Planes shot at him from above and antiaircraft guns from below, but he somehow managed to hit the ground unharmed. He found himself in a farmer's field. He buried his flight suit and his parachute and spent the next three days on the run, sleeping in hedgerows during the day, eating raw potatoes from farmers' fields, and traveling at night.

Germans swarmed all over the area, searching for him and anyone else who managed to survive the jump.

"That first night I heard trucks on the road and dove into a ditch. One of them stopped and eight or ten Germans got out and started to hunt for me. I pressed myself so far down into that ditch that I ended up with a mouthful of dirt," he said. "It took every bit of grit I had not to get up and run. I crept forward on my belly like a snake." He shook his head in amazement. "I still can't figure how they didn't catch me, but they didn't, and I sure am glad.

"I didn't know where I was going," Steve said. "I just knew I had to keep moving. On my third night I snuck up behind a farmhouse. I was going to try and steal something to eat from the garden or the barn, but I could see a family through the window sitting down to supper. I smelled hot food and the people looked nice, so I went ahead and knocked on the door.

"'American,' I said, when the farmer answered. I had a French phrase card in my escape kit, so I knew how to say 'please help me.' The old man yelled like crazy, but his wife shushed him and pulled me inside. I spent one night there. They fed me and let me sleep on the kitchen floor. Then the next morning another man showed up. He led me to a depot and someone else took me on a train to Paris. When I got here, your friend Fox led me through the train station and out onto the street. Next thing I knew I was here."

Steve was anxious to leave France. He was tired of being cooped up in that small room, not able to walk, not able to talk to his host. He knew he was putting her life in danger. The penalty for men who got caught helping an enemy aviator was death by firing squad. Women were sent to concentration camps, which was only a slower form of death.

Finally, the doctor brought a cane and said Steve could walk, but he had to build up his muscles and his stamina before he could think about hiking over the Pyrenees into Spain. I took him out for walks—at first just to the corner and back, but soon we were walking around the block and going farther and farther. At first, we both tensed up every time we saw a Nazi soldier, but they weren't interested in men with canes. Soon we relaxed and even enjoyed our walks together, even though we couldn't risk speaking out loud. I had to break him of his habit of keeping one hand in his pocket and jingling the coins he carried. That was something Frenchmen never did.

On his final morning in Paris, I took Steve on a tour of the sights. He tried not to look too much like a tourist when I walked him by the Eiffel Tower and Napoleon's Tomb. Then I led him to the *Gare d'Austerlitz*, where someone else would lead him onto a train and into the South of France. From there, he would hike over the Pyrenees mountains into Spain.

I spotted his contact. A young woman in a red suit—a rare spot of color in what had become a very gray city. I nodded in her direction. Steve looked me in the eye for a moment and walked toward her.

We had said our good-byes before we left his safe house.

"I would have gone crazy without your company," he told me. "And I wouldn't have gotten strong enough to leave without our long walks."

I shrugged off his thanks, but the truth was that I was going to miss Steve Jones. He treated me like an equal, not a boy. He was interested in me and what I had to say, even though I

couldn't tell him very much about myself. "I'm doing my duty," I told him. "I'm proud to help."

"And I'm proud to know you, Wolfie," Steve said. "Is there anyone you want me to get in touch with when I get back to England? I could get word to your family in the States."

My eyes widened. How did he know I had family in the States. Had I slipped up?

Steve laughed. "Just a guess, Wolfie. Just a guess."

I smiled. I wanted him to get word to Papa about the work I was doing. I wanted it desperately. But it was too dangerous. "There's no one," I said. "Except Hitler. Drop a bomb on him for me."

★ CHAPTER SIXTEEN ★

"Newspaper, *Monsieur?*"

May 1943

After Steve Jones left, François finally put me to work guiding aviators around Paris. Trains from Belgium and northern France arrived at the *Gare du Nord*. I led the men to safe houses in Paris, or to the *Gare d'Austerlitz*. From there, another *résistant* led them on a train south—the jumping-off point for the hike into Spain.

Jacques led me on my first few missions, as he had before. He carried one newspaper under his arm, a pro-German propaganda rag. When the train pulled into the station, Jacques waited calmly. He elbowed me in the side as two men

got off the train. I knew immediately which one was the aviator. He didn't have the pinched, sullen look of a man who had lived under German occupation for three years. I memorized the contact's face. I would be seeing it again, and a mistake could be fatal.

The two men walked down the platform.

Jacques sauntered toward the guide. "Newspaper, *monsieur*?" he asked. "It's my last one."

The guide took the paper and handed it to his friend. The exchange had been made.

Jacques headed into the station with me on his heels. The guide and the aviator drifted apart as if they didn't know each other at all. I kept checking to make sure the aviator was following us. We passed through the Nazi checkpoint leading out of the station. My heart fluttered like crazy. What if the Nazi guards asked the aviator a question? I held my breath, waiting. But the guard gave the aviator's papers only a quick glance and waved him on.

"Stop looking back," Jacques muttered. He pointed to a window on the other side of the street. "Look there."

I saw my reflection in the window glass. The aviator was coming up behind us.

Once we were on stairs leading down to the *métro*, Jacques turned to me and asked, "Have you done your homework?"

"Homework?" I asked. But Jacques had already turned around again. He was simply checking to make sure the aviator was still there.

I noticed that the aviator kept his face buried in his newspaper on the *métro*, peering over the top of it now and then. When we were near our stop, Jacques stood and moved to the door. The aviator did the same. We got off in the Marais neighborhood. Jacques headed across the street, into an apartment building, and up the stairs to an apartment on the fourth floor. A man I had never seen before answered, speaking through a crack in the door. "How's the newspaper business today?" he asked

"I sold my last one," Jacques told him.

The aviator and I both practically fell into the apartment when the man opened the door all the way. I'm not sure which one of us was more relieved.

From that day on, I was a guide. Sometimes Jacques and I worked together and sometimes each of us worked alone. My favorite thing to do was lead the men to one of the two safe houses we used. There I could talk to them about what was going on in the rest of the world, and ask when the Allies were going to invade France. The British and the Americans all had the same answer:

"We're gearing up for a massive invasion, but we don't know when or where it will happen."

Some of them still had their escape kits. They flew with photographs ready to paste into fake identity cards, tiny compasses and silk maps, tablets to help them stay awake for twenty-four hours, and money for all the countries they flew over. Sometimes they even had chocolate bars. The Americans thought of everything.

The most dangerous missions were the ones in which I had to lead the pilots from one train station to the other without a stop at a safe house. The Nazis watched the train stations more carefully than they did the *métro*, and there were hours to fill in between trains. Once I led an aviator to a café only to remember that American men ate differently from French men. They held their forks in their right hands and did an awkward dance with the knife whenever they had to cut something. I spent the whole meal worried that a German would wander in.

One Saturday I had too many hours in between trains—too much time to safely wait at the station. I led my aviator into a movie theater. We sat in the dark, far from the other patrons, whispering in English. Then, suddenly, the movie stopped and the lights went on. Nazis poured into the theater and blocked the exits. They interrogated every man over eighteen. If they didn't have the proper papers, they were arrested and transported to German war factories.

My eyes darted around the theater looking for an escape. There was none. My aviator looked young and healthy—exactly the kind of man the Germans wanted. I pulled my ID card out of my pocket and motioned to him to do the same. He had a small pile of papers. I flipped through them quickly. The aviator had French-army discharge papers, one of which said he was disabled. I could only hope it was a good enough forgery.

I handed the aviator his papers just before the *boche* got to us. He barely looked at my documents before turning to my new friend.

"Papers," the Nazi demanded.

The aviator turned them over. He kept his eyes trained on the movie screen and not on the Nazi soldier.

The Nazi stared at them for a long minute. He

flipped from the discharge papers to the identity card and read and reread the disability form. Finally, after what felt like an hour, he shoved the papers back into the man's hands and moved on.

We dropped into our seats—both of us gulping for air. That was the only time I brought an aviator to the movies. From then on I made sure to stay on the move. I was always relieved when it was time to turn them over to the next guide.

Maman and I had only one conversation about my work during this time. She knew I had gotten involved in the Resistance again. I was disappearing for longer and longer periods of time. One day, when I got home from dropping off an aviator at the train station, she was waiting at the door.

"Tell me what you're up to," she said.

"It's better if you don't know."

She waited for me to say more.

"It's important," I said. "And it's necessary."

"Are you putting yourself in danger?"

Was I? I shrugged and looked away.

Maman sighed. "Are you putting Charlotte or me in any danger?"

"No," I said. I believed it. With the exception of Jacques and his brother, no one in the Resistance knew my name or where I lived. Even the aviators. So many times I wanted to write a letter to Papa and slip it to one of them, but it was too dangerous. A captured letter would lead the Gestapo right to our door.

"The real danger comes if the Nazis win," I told her. "I'm not doing anything risky."

Maman brushed my hair out of my eyes. "You've turned into a little man. I'm sorry you didn't get to be a boy for a few years longer. I'm proud of you."

Would Papa be proud too? I wondered. I had continued to add rungs to the ladder in my imagination, but I wasn't sure if it would ever be tall enough. At least he could not say that I had put Maman and Charlotte in danger.

But then I did. I had no choice.

CHAPTER SEVENTEEN

"Bone Joor"

August 1943

Every time I saw an Allied plane in the sky, I worried about how we would get the aviators to safety if it crashed. One afternoon I was with Jacques and François in their apartment when the air-raid sirens sounded. Instead of heading for shelter, we went to the roof to see what we could see.

I recognized the planes as the kind Steve Jones had flown—Flying Fortresses. They were heading to the suburbs west of Paris.

"They're going to bomb the factories," François said. "The Germans turned them into war plants."

We were close enough to watch bombs drop from the bellies of the planes and black smoke rise from the ground. Puffs from German antiaircraft guns spiraled up. I cringed each time one of the Allied planes got hit. Some came down in flames. We could see aviators jumping like dots in the sky. Some of the parachutes were on fire. Bodies hurtled toward the earth. Other airmen dangled from their floating clouds, helpless to protect themselves while guns shot at them from below.

I took comfort that at least some of the men would make it into the hands of the Resistance instead of the Nazis'.

That night we were able to tune into the BBC for the French news. The announcer was cool and impersonal. "American bombers attacked targets in the western suburbs of Paris today. Sixteen bombers are missing."

I tried to remember what Steve had told me about the crew on those planes. There were eight or nine men on every single one of them. "Sixteen planes," I said to Jacques. "That's more than a hundred and twenty-five men."

"Where will we find food, clothes, and safe houses for that many?" Jacques asked.

The Resistance was struggling to take care

of the aviators who wanted to escape to Spain, but Jacques and I only had to worry about one man at a time. The next afternoon, we headed to the *Gare du Nord* to pick up an aviator. This one wouldn't spend the night in a safe house, but head directly to the *Gare d'Austerlitz*.

Our man got off the last car, along with his guide. The aviator carried a small suitcase. Sometimes they posed as Frenchmen on a business trip. This one was older than most—old enough to pull that off. I approached the two of them with my newspaper. "Newspaper, *monsieur?*" I asked. "It's my last copy."

The guide handed me a coin. The aviator took the newspaper.

"Bonne chance," the guide whispered. "Good luck." He kissed the aviator on both cheeks and disappeared into the crowd.

I followed Jacques through the busy train station and into the café, trusting the man to stay behind us. We had learned that we could avoid the Nazi checkpoints by going through the restaurant. We would pretend to look for a table, and then change our minds.

"Let's go home," Jacques said. "My *maman* made rabbit stew."

I nodded and followed him through the café's street door and onto the avenue. No Nazi checkpoint in sight.

Jacques and I crossed the busy street, weaving in and out of bicycles and pedestrians. I checked our reflections in the windows on the other side of the street as Jacques had showed me. The American appeared to be struggling.

"Slow down," I said to Jacques. "We have plenty of time."

He slowed a bit, but when I looked over my shoulder, I saw that the pilot had stopped. He was clutching his suitcase in one hand and using the other to hold on to the side of a building. I could see his chest rising and falling, as if he couldn't get enough air. Was he too frightened to continue? His knees buckled and he crumpled to the sidewalk.

"Jacques, wait!" I said.

Jacques turned. His eyes widened and then he shook his head. He was right, of course. One English word out of the man's mouth and we would all get arrested—and shot by a firing squad.

I looked back. A man was kneeling over the aviator, fanning his face.

Jacques grabbed my arm and tried to drag me to the *métro*. "It's too dangerous," he hissed.

"I can't," I said. "I can't leave him."

"Fine," Jacques said. "I'm going."

For a minute I stood between the two of them. Going with Jacques was the safe thing to do, but I couldn't leave an American lying on the sidewalk for the Nazis. I watched Jacques get swallowed up by the people hurrying to the *métro* and rushed back to the man.

A small crowd had gathered. I pushed through them to kneel by the aviator's side. I made sure to put a hand on his suitcase. I didn't know what was in it, but I was afraid there was something that would give him away.

He was lying on his back. It wasn't fear that had made him collapse. He was burning up with fever.

The crowd was getting bigger. Any one of them could turn us in to the Gestapo for some coal or a couple of eggs. The *boches* didn't like crowds— they saw every gathering of French people as a possible plot against them. It was seconds before one of them pushed his way into the center of this one to see what was happening.

"*Was ist los?*" he demanded in German.

The man who had first come to the aviator's aide murmured to the soldier in German. Then he pointed to me. I think he said the German word for son. That gave me an idea.

"Papa, Papa, you fainted," I said quickly in French. "*Ne parles pas,*" I hoped the aviator would understand French for "don't talk." I didn't dare say the words in English.

The Nazi asked me a question in German I did not understand. "He's sick. I must get him home," I said.

The man who said the aviator was my father hailed a bicycle taxi. "I'll help you," he said, positioning himself between the aviator and the Nazi. "*Américain?*" he whispered.

I panicked. How did he know?

"Your *papa* will be fine," he said, more loudly. "He needs to rest." The man said something in German to the Nazi, and helped me walk my "*papa*" to the taxi. The aviator slumped into the seat and I climbed in next to him with the suitcase.

The man slipped a few francs into my hand.

"*Merci, monsieur,*" I said. "I am very grateful."

He waved me off and told the driver to hurry

away. "Take good care of your *papa,*" he said. "Very good care."

The driver pedaled away like he was told. Only then did I realize how smart the helpful man was—he made sure we got away from the Nazi soldier before I had to give the driver an address.

When we reached the corner, he slowed down. "Where to?" he asked.

Where to? The American couldn't get on a train, not in his condition. Both safe houses were over-loaded. I didn't think they'd be willing to take in a sick man—doing that would risk the health and safely of the other aviators and their guides. I didn't know what else to do, so I gave the driver my own address.

By the time we got there, the man had revived enough to walk on his own. Madame Cassou, as always, was at her concierge window.

"Our cousin from the south," I said. "Here for a visit."

Thank goodness the elevator was working— I didn't think the man could handle the stairs. I got him inside and into Georges's bed.

"You're going to be fine," I told him.

He nodded. "Thank you," he mumbled, and drifted off to sleep.

A couple of hours later, I greeted Maman and Charlotte when they came through the door. Maman took one look at my face and knew something was wrong. "What is it?" she asked.

I led her to Georges's room. "An American aviator," I said. "Sick."

The man opened his eyes, saw Maman, and tried to get to his feet. "Bone joor," he said.

Maman pushed past me. "I'm American too," she said. "Get back into bed before you fall and hurt yourself."

★ CHAPTER EIGHTEEN ★

The New York Dodgers

August 1943

The doctor said the man had pneumonia. There was nothing he could do. The Germans guarded hospitals and pharmacies so closely that he couldn't bring the sick man any medicine. We had to wait and hope he would get better with rest and food. Maman and I took turns nursing him.

For the first two days, his fever burned so hot that I was afraid he was going to die. He thrashed around muttering to crewmen only he could see. Every once in a while he would sit bolt upright.

"Watch out! Messerschmitt at twelve o'clock," he'd yell. Or he'd give the order to jump. "Bail out! Bail out!" Then he'd drop back onto the mattress, exhausted and terrified. "My fault," he muttered over and over. "My fault."

When I asked François what we would do if the man died, he merely shrugged. "A dead aviator will be a lot harder to move out of Paris than a live one," he said. "Let's hope he lives."

A couple of days later, the aviator's fever broke. The worst was over.

By the end of the week Second Lieutenant Charles "Mack" Mackey from Pennsylvania was able to sit up and feed himself. Unlike Steve Jones and some of the other aviators, Mack wasn't eager to tell his story. We learned only the most basic of details. He was a pilot and he was shot down over Belgium. It had taken him weeks to get from Belgium to Paris, but no one on the escape line was able to tell him anything about the members of his crew. He was desperate to find out if any of them had survived the jump and made it into the hands of the Resistance. He recited their names to me over and over, asking me to check.

I recognized his need for answers. I felt that way when Georges was first arrested. Mack felt responsible for his crew like I felt responsible for Georges's arrest.

When I dropped aviators at the safe house in the Marais, I asked the man whom I knew only as Hippo.

"No one keeps such a list," he told me. "Too dangerous."

I recited the names for him, but he didn't recognize any of them.

"I almost never know their names," he said. "Or I forget as soon as you bring me a new one."

Every time I went out and came back in again, Mack turned to me with a hopeful look. Each time I had to shake my head in a silent no and watch Mack's hope melt into disappointment. His health improved but his spirits didn't.

Maman did not share Mack's shyness or the Resistance's caution. She told him all about her family on Long Island, about Papa in England, and about Georges in Germany. He told her all about his wife and children in Pennsylvania. It wasn't long before Mack was calling me Michael instead of the Wolf.

"Maman, it's dangerous for him to know so much about us," I told her.

Maman waved me off. "The man needs to talk about his family."

"Yes, but you're telling him too much about

us. What if he gets picked up by the Gestapo?"

I think it was only then that Maman recognized the danger we were in, but it was too late. I knew I had to send Mack on his journey as soon as he was strong enough to leave.

In the meantime, I helped other aviators whenever I was given a mission. One day in early October, François asked me to meet him on the roof. "I need you to talk to someone," he said. "Make sure he's really American."

"What do you mean?"

"Nazis spies pretend to be downed aviators," he said. "We have a man who says he's American, but England can't back up his claim."

The Resistance checked out every single aviator to make sure they were real Allies and not Nazi spies. Radio operators communicated with England using small radios and Morse code. The Nazis had special trucks that picked up the radio signals and rushed to arrest the *résistants*. It was one of the most dangerous jobs in the Resistance. Radio operators were constantly on the run.

"Talk to the man about America," François said. "See what you think."

The idea scared me. How would I know for sure? But François was still a little mad at me for bringing Mack home. I needed to make up for that. I slipped an American novel of Maman's into a rucksack and took the *métro* to the safe house. When I got there, I checked to make sure our signal, an ivy plant, was in the window. Then I climbed the stairs.

The Hippo met me in the hall. "There's something not right about this one."

"What will you do if he's a Nazi?" I asked.

"Interrogate him and then—" The Hippo ran his finger across his throat.

One Nazi spy could lead to hundreds of arrests. I understood that the man would have to die, but what if I was wrong?

"Ready?" he asked.

I wasn't, but I pretended to be. "Ready."

He ushered me into the apartment and led me to the back room where the aviators slept. The man had opened the curtains and the window. He was leaning out, breathing in the fresh air. I was immediately on alert. A man in hiding—even a stupid man—didn't do such things.

The Hippo rushed to the window and pulled the curtains closed.

"Sorry," the man said sheepishly in English. "I haven't been outside in days."

"Soon. Soon you go south," the Hippo said in his broken English. He turned to me and switched to French. "Introduce yourself."

"Hello," I said. "I'm the Wolf."

"You're American?" he asked.

I made sure my answer was vague. "I was there once or twice."

"Bob Jackson," he said shaking my hand. "From New York City."

I forced myself to smile. "I've been to New York City," I said.

Hippo left the room. Bob and I talked about the sights in New York—the Empire State Building and Radio City Music Hall. Everything seemed to be correct. Then I asked him about my favorite American sport. I never could get my French friends interested playing, but before the war I followed the baseball teams on the radio. One of my uncles loved the Yankees. The other one rooted for the Dodgers. I loved to watch them argue about which team was better.

"I saw a baseball game when I was in New York before the war," I said. "Do you have a favorite team?"

"Of course," the aviator said. "The New York Dodgers."

It was the *Brooklyn* Dodgers, everyone knew that.

I was instantly on alert. Bob stiffened. Did he sense my distrust?

"Aha," I said, pretending to laugh. "Then you are my enemy. I am a Yankee fan."

"I'll take you to a game after the war," he said. "You'll see whose team is better."

"I went to a game at the Yankee Stadium in Brooklyn," I said. "Have you ever been there?" Anyone from New York would know that Yankee Stadium was in the Bronx, not Brooklyn.

"No," he answered with a smile. "I'm a Dodger man through and through."

I lowered my head so that he would not see my face. He was opening and closing his hands. Was he going to strangle me? "My uncle likes the Chicago Red Sox," I said.

I saw confusion cross the man's face. I waited for him to tell me the Red Sox were from Boston. He didn't.

"Did I get that right?" I asked. "The *Chicago* Red Sox? I always get the cities confused."

"Yes," he said with a firm nod. "The Chicago Red Sox. But the New York Dodgers are a better team."

New York again, not Brooklyn. It's one thing not to like baseball, but *everyone* knows it's the

Brooklyn Dodgers. Especially someone who pretended to be a baseball fan.

"I have to go," I said, "but I have something for you." I pulled the book out of my rucksack and gripped it so that he would not see that my hands were trembling. "Something to read until you can get away."

He took it from me and read the title. *"Of Mice and Men,"* he said. Then he looked up with a smile. "Who is the mouse and who is the man?" he asked.

I didn't answer. His words felt like a threat. If I was the mouse, then he was the trap. I couldn't wait to get out of that room. "Good-bye."

"Good-bye," he said. "I'll see you again."

I nodded and left. I found Hippo in the living room with a couple of men I hadn't seen before. He held a finger to his lips and then raised his hands in a question.

I didn't say a word. I ran my finger across my throat the same way he had earlier. My hand was shaking. That motion, so simple, would lead to a man's death.

I tossed and turned all night. If I was wrong about Bob Jackson, an innocent man—an American man—would die. But if he was a Nazi and they let him go, my comrades in the Resistance would die.

The next afternoon after school, I headed to the safe house to find out what had happened. Jacques offered to come with me, but I told him to go home. If there was danger, I wanted to face it alone.

There was a Nazi truck and two black Mercedes on the street in front of the apartment building. The plant in the window had been knocked over. I tried to tell myself that that didn't mean anything either. But it did.

Two seconds later I watched soldiers drag the Hippo and the two other men out of the building. Behind them was Bob Jackson, his face a mass of bruises. He was arm in arm with the Gestapo. I didn't wait for him to see me. I ran.

★ CHAPTER NINETEEN ★

Gestapo

October 1943

I was desperate to warn François and Jacques about what I had seen. I ran all the way home. I stopped short when I saw two more black Mercedes in front of our apartment building. Two soldiers were leaning casually against the cars, chatting. They were regular soldiers, but those cars were unmistakable: Gestapo.

I was watching from the corner when the soldiers jumped to attention and saluted before opening the car doors. I held my breath.

Seconds later I watched a Gestapo officer drag Jacques and François out of the building.

No!

It couldn't be.

I wanted to scream, but I clamped a hand over my mouth, keeping the words inside.

François was talking quickly. I was too far away to hear, but he seemed to be pleading. Jacques's eyes were on his feet. There was as stain on the front of his pants and I wondered what the Gestapo had done to make him wet himself. I felt a wave of sympathy for my friend, for how frightened he must be.

The officer threw the brothers into the back-seat of the first car. Jacques's head hit the roof and he staggered, but the officer only pushed him hard. Then he slammed the door and gave what sounded like an order to the driver. Another Gestapo officer led Jacques's parents to the second car. Mrs. Dubois was crying. Mr. Dubois stared straight ahead.

I stepped back into the shadows of a doorway and watched the cars speed past. My whole body was shaking and I fought not to cry. I had to think. My survival—my family's survival—depended on my staying calm and coming up with a plan.

A German or a *collabo* had managed to worm his way into the escape line again. It wouldn't matter how much evidence the Nazis had. François and Jacques would go before a German military judge and be sent to prison or to a firing squad. Did the Nazis kill children? Jacques had just turned thirteen. François was sixteen. And what about their parents? They were innocent, but the Nazis didn't care. What was better, a quick death at the end of a Nazi rifle or a long, slow death in prison?

I stamped my foot in rage, then took a deep, shaky breath. Anger was better than fear. Anger stopped my trembling, but I still had to come up with a plan. Jacques and François were the only two members of our resistance cell who knew my real name and where I lived. How long would it be before one of them broke under torture and gave me away?

Now I knew who was the mouse. Me. And I was caught in a trap. How long before the Gestapo showed up to finish me off?

Stop! I said to myself. *Stop and think.*

The first thing I had to do was make sure Maman and Charlotte were all right, and Mack too. I took a few more deep breaths and then stepped out of the doorway and onto the sidewalk. I wanted to run, but I forced myself to walk at a normal pace. Showing fear right now would only make me seem suspicious.

I tried to whistle a tune as I sauntered up to my building, but my mouth was too dry.

Madame Cassou was at her concierge window, as always, keeping an eye on everything that happened. Collecting gossip. She waved me over.

"Gestapo," she said. "They just left."

I pretended to be surprised. "Again?" I asked. "I thought they were satisfied that Maman wasn't an American spy." I forced myself to laugh.

"Not your maman. Your friends—the Duboises. *Résistants*," she said.

"No! I'm sure it's just a misunderstanding," I told her.

She cocked an eyebrow. How much did she know? Had she been the one to turn us in?

I kept on pretending and headed for the stairs. "They'll be back later today—like my family was when the Gestapo took us in for questioning," I said over my shoulder. As soon as I was out of her sight, I ran. I took the stairs two at a time.

When I got to my floor, I heard German voices coming from the floor above, along with crashing sounds. They were searching Jacques's apartment, looking for evidence. Was there anything that would lead them to me?

I tried my own door and it was locked. I knocked softly, afraid to be heard by the men upstairs.

Maman answered and pulled me to her. "You're safe," she said, burying her nose in my hair. I felt her tears on my head.

"They got Jacques's family," I said.

She nodded and wiped her eyes. "I know."

Mack walked into the room. He had a rucksack over his shoulders. "I'm going to leave," he said, "before I cause any more trouble. I'll make my way to the train station and take my chances. I'll get south to the mountains somehow."

"Don't be silly," Maman said. "You're not strong enough, and you don't speak the language."

"I've already put you in too much danger," he said.

"We all have to leave," I told him. I hadn't known that this was true until I said the words. But we couldn't stay in Paris. If I wasn't here, the Gestapo would still arrest Maman. "It's just a matter of time before someone cracks under torture, or identifies a photo of me. Who knows how long the *boches* have been watching, waiting to arrest us all."

Maman let out a cry.

I had never seen her look so scared or so desperate—not even when I told her about Georges's
arrest. I had caused this, and now I had to come
up with a plan to save her and Charlotte. If I
thought any one of those Nazis had a heart, I'd
throw myself on their mercy and tell them anything they wanted to know if they'd let Maman
and Charlotte go. But they had no hearts.

Was there anyone left in my resistance group?
I didn't know where false identity papers came
from, but if I could get my hands on a set for Maman and Charlotte, they could get away. Hide out
in a small village where no one knew them. I had
memorized the phone number of the safe house
in the Pigalle in case of an emergency. The Germans listened in on phone calls, so I had to be
careful. At least I'd know if the people there were
still free, and I could alert them to the danger.

I picked up our phone and dialed the number.
I came up with something that would let them
know there was trouble, without giving myself
away. I decided to tell whoever answered that his
cousin was very ill and take it from there.

But it didn't matter what I said, because my comrades didn't answer. A German did. *"Ja? Ja?"* he said.

I slammed the phone down.

★ CHAPTER TWENTY ★

On the Run

Maman jumped when I hung up the phone. I didn't want her to see that I was starting to panic. I turned my back and ran through a mental list of people we knew in Paris, trying to figure out who might take us in for a few days. Then I dismissed that idea. It would be too dangerous to get any of our friends mixed up in our troubles. And what would I tell them about Mack?

Charlotte walked down the hall then, followed by one of my rabbits. She was always sneaking off to play with them, trying to turn them into pets. Uncle Henri said she'd never make a good farmer's wife. That's when it hit me—Uncle Henri would know what to do.

He made no secret of his hatred for the *boches;* he had hated them ever since the last war. If there was a resistance group in Jouy, then Uncle Henri was at the center of it. And if there wasn't one already, he would start one. There had to be more than one underground escape line in France, and it wouldn't surprise me one bit if Uncle Henri knew exactly how I could get Mack to Spain.

The more I thought about it, the more I believed he was our answer. "Uncle Henri," I said to Maman. "Uncle Henri will help us."

"Yes, he will," she said, "but to involve him . . ."

"He would want us to come. I'm sure of it."

Maman hesitated.

"He's our best choice," I said.

"All right," Maman agreed. "We'll go. If nothing else, they can take Charlotte if—"

She couldn't finish the sentence, but I knew what she meant. If we get arrested.

Mack looked from one to the other of us, waiting for an explanation.

"My uncle in the country—a farmer," I explained. "I'm sure he's in the Resistance."

We quickly packed a few things in our rucksacks. Maman hid her money and jewelry in the false bottom of her shopping bag, and we wore extra clothes. We would be overly warm, but winter would come soon enough. And where would we be then? I wondered.

The Hippo had once told me about a hotel that didn't ask for identity cards. It was near the *Gare du Nord*, and he thought I might need it for an aviator one day. We decided to spend the night there, rather than in our apartment, and catch the morning train to the country.

It was Monday. Five days until Maman had to register at the police station. The Gestapo would come looking for us then, if not before. I'm sure the Nazis knew Papa had a brother in the country. They seemed to know everything. Was there a way to make them believe we had gone somewhere else?

Only one solution came to mind. When Maman, Charlotte, and Mack got on the train to Uncle Henri's, I would have to stay behind, and leave a false trail for the Nazis.

I didn't tell Maman. The next morning we all went to the *Gare du Nord* together. When I bought the tickets, I only paid for three. When the train pulled into the station, I told Maman my plan.

"I'm going south," I said. "I'll mail a postcard to the concierge from somewhere and tell her our plans changed and we decided to stay with our cousins for a few weeks. I'll ask her to take care of the rabbits," I told her. "It might delay the Nazis by a day or two."

"No!" Maman grabbed my arm and tried to pull me onto the train, but I pulled back.

Charlotte started to cry and that drew some attention to us.

Maman couldn't yell. She couldn't force me to board. Too much attention could lead to our arrest. And she couldn't stay with me. She had to get Charlotte and Mack to the country.

I took another step backward and waved happily for the benefit of anyone who was watching. "I'll see you soon," I said. "Don't cry, Charlotte. I'll see you soon."

Mack couldn't say anything without giving himself away, but he put one hand on Maman's shoulder and wrapped the other around Charlotte. He was letting me know he would take care of them. I watched the train chug away, and tried not to think that I might never see them again.

I walked through the café to leave the train station, as I had so many times with the aviators.

Then I took the *métro* to the *Gare d'Austerlitz* and bought a ticket on the first train going south. I got off at Orléans.

The Orléans train station was swarming with Nazis. There were checkpoints at every turn. Was my name on a list? Were they already looking for me? There was nothing to do but hand over my papers. My hands were shaking, but the soldier didn't notice. He gave my identity card a quick glance and nodded to me to go on.

I got away from the train station as quickly as possible. Orléans wasn't as big as Paris, but it was a busy city. I stopped at a café and asked for directions to the nearest post office. I bought a postcard and a stamp and wrote a note to Madame Cassou:

> *We have decided to stay with my cousin*
> *in Orléans for a few weeks. Please take*
> *care of my rabbits.*
> *Sincerely,*
> *Michael Durand*

I knew her well enough to know that Madame Cassou would eat a few and sell a few as her payment for watching them. I couldn't return to our apartment in Paris until after the war was over and the Nazis were gone.

Was an Orléans postmark enough to throw them off our trail?

I wandered around the city for a few hours. I didn't want to go back to the train station and all those Nazis, but eventually I had to. I made the return trip, arriving in Paris just before curfew.

I stepped out onto the street with no idea of where to go. Jacques had been arrested. My home wasn't safe. I didn't have money to go back to the hotel. I couldn't be caught on the street after curfew, and a night in the train station would only lead to questions from the police.

I expected to find the Gestapo lying in wait at every corner. The streetlamps, painted blue because of the blackout, cast an creepy glow, but they also made me less visible in the dark. Finally, about halfway between the two train stations, I huddled in a dark doorway. I was hungry and cold, and I felt completely alone in the world. Even so, I knew I was lucky. Wherever Jacques was right now, he was much more frightened and much more alone than I was.

★ CHAPTER TWENTY-ONE ★

Uncle Henri

Each time I dropped off to sleep, a nightmare woke me. I was awake when I heard Nazi boots stomping down the street. *At least you can always count on the Nazis to be loud,* I thought. I huddled into an even tighter ball and prayed they wouldn't see me. The noise got closer and closer. My head was buried in my knees and I had to bite my tongue to keep from screaming.

I waited for one of them to shout and the others to come running. But after a few minutes the noise moved farther away again. I spent the rest of the night sitting bolt upright, holding my eyelids open with my fingers whenever I felt myself dropping off to sleep.

As soon as it was light, I ran to the *Gare du Nord* and bought my train ticket, then I made my way to the café and bought a coffee with the few francs I had left. I didn't like coffee, especially the fake acorn coffee that was served since the war began. Today I thought it might wake me up. The waiter did a double take when he saw me. Was my picture on a wanted poster? I steeled myself to run, but he only brought me a piece of fake, straw-filled bread to go with my fake coffee. I guess I looked as hungry as I felt.

When I finished, I hid in the bathroom until it was time for the train.

My eyes darted all over the platform, waiting for someone to yell, "There he is! Arrest him!" I had spent a lot of time on this platform waiting for aviators. I had always been lucky, always managed to get my men safely to their next stop on the escape line. Would my luck hold out today?

I kept checking over my shoulder to make sure I wasn't being watched. Jacques would tell me to stop, that I was being too obvious. But I couldn't help myself. Everyone looked German, pretending to be French.

Was the man at the other end of the platform watching me over the top of his newspaper? What about the bored-looking farmer? Or the woman in the blue hat? The train pulled in and I waited until the very last moment to jump on board. Then I slumped into a seat and said a silent good-bye to Paris.

I wanted to stay awake, but the motion of the train rocked me to sleep. My nightmares returned. The conductor jiggled my arm to wake me, and I jumped to my feet, screaming.

"Your stop is next," he told me.

I took deep gulps of air and nodded my thanks. In my dream, Jacques had been in front of a firing squad, staring into the barrel of a rifle.

I wandered through the village, trying to look as if I belonged there and be invisible at the same time. It was a crisp fall day and the air smelled of hay and sunshine. I strolled past the hotel and the tobacco store, the grocery, the bakery, the butcher, the church. It looked much like it would have before the war—if you didn't look at the store shelves and notice they were mostly bare. And the flag flying over the town hall was Nazi, not French.

I walked in the direction of Uncle Henri's farm.

I considered circling around and approaching the farmhouse through the fields, just in case the Nazis were lying in wait. But I was too tired, and too sad about Jacques and François and everyone else—all those people whose names I didn't know who worked together in secret to battle the Nazis and save American and British aviators.

I thought I was doing the right thing for France, but I had put my family in danger. I listened for Papa's voice in my head, but it was silent. Perhaps I was beyond even Papa's disapproval now.

That ladder I had built, rung by rung, to win his respect had come toppling down like matchsticks in the wind.

I trudged up the lane to the farmhouse. The farm smelled just like it always had—like wheat and hay and rabbits. Charlotte was in the yard, feeding the chickens and singing a song. I was about to call to her when Uncle Henri ran out of the barn.

"He's here!" he shouted. "Louise, he's here."

Mack was right behind him.

Maman and Aunt Jeanne ran out of the house.

We all came together in the yard. Maman and Aunt Jeanne were hugging me and crying. Charlotte threw her arms around my legs. Uncle Henri kept patting me on the back and saying, "You're here. You made it. That's good."

"Thank goodness, you're safe," Maman said, wiping away tears.

Mack stood back and took it all in, blinking away tears. I'm sure he had no idea what anyone was saying.

"You must be hungry," Aunt Jeanne said. She pulled me into the kitchen and sat me at the table before filling a bowl with a thick and delicious chicken stew. There was bread, and real butter. Butter! I hadn't seen real butter in a very long time.

I told them my story between bites—about going to Orléans and spending the night in Paris before catching the train this morning.

"Have you heard anything about what happened in Paris?" I asked Uncle Henri.

He shook his head. "Only that there were many arrests. The *boches* are coming down hard on us. They're losing the war, and that makes them angry."

I noticed that he said *us*. I knew my uncle would be one of us—one of the Resistance. He didn't seem at all surprised that I was working with the Resistance either, or that I was helping American and English aviators.

"Mack has to get to Spain somehow," I said. "And Maman, Charlotte, and I will need new identity papers and a place to stay. The *boches* will look for us here when they realize we've left Paris. We need to be gone before they come."

Uncle Henri nodded seriously. "All will be taken care of. Your friend"—he nodded in Mack's direction—"can leave by plane tomorrow night."

My jaw dropped. Could it possibly be that easy? "By plane?"

"If all goes well, the English will fly in on Thursday. There are three operatives coming in from England, and two spies who must go back. It's rare they pick up aviators, but there's a spot on the plane."

I sat back, stunned. There were parts of the Resistance I knew nothing about. "What about forged papers for the rest of us?"

"That will be harder," my uncle told me. "The Germans are watching everything very carefully. Paper, ink, even typewriter ribbons. It may take time, but we'll get them."

"But the Gestapo—"

"Don't worry about the Gestapo now," Aunt Jeanne told me. "Eat. And rest. Tomorrow we will worry about the Gestapo."

Uncle Henri must have hidden other *résistants* on the farm. Mack and I slept in the hayloft, where my uncle had created a secret compartment under the floorboards. We could scoot in there pretty easily if the Nazis showed up. It was dark and cramped, but it would do. For Maman and Charlotte, there was a secret spot in the cellar. We'd survive a search, as long as it wasn't too thorough.

The next morning, my uncle's friend came to go over the details of the plane landing. He was much younger than Uncle Henri—young enough to be picked up by a German patrol and forced to work in a war factory. But everything about him said "farmer," from the sunburn on his face to the manure on his shoes. In these hungry times, farmers were just as important to the German cause as bullets.

He explained that everything had to go just right. "You are very lucky, *mon ami*," he said to Mack in a mixture of English and French. "There is room on the plane for one more man. You came at just the right time."

"I'm grateful," Mack said.

"Go back to your plane and drop bombs on the Germans," my uncle said, asking me to translate. "Tell the Allies that they have to hurry and invade France. The woods are full of young men who are hiding from the Germans. We're ready to fight, but we can't do it alone."

Mack promised to do what he could.

Then I asked Uncle Henri's contact about false papers for Maman, Charlotte, and me. He said the same thing as Uncle Henri. "We can get them, but it will take time."

Time was something we didn't have. In two days, the police would alert the Gestapo that Maman had not come in to register—that is if Jacques and François didn't turn us in before then.

Was my friend being tortured? If Jacques was in enough pain, would he say anything to get them to stop?

CHAPTER TWENTY-TWO

Night Flight

I began to formulate a plan of my own—a plan to get Maman and Charlotte to a safe place where they wouldn't need false papers. I shared it with Mack and waited for him to agree. I couldn't do it without him. He thought about it for a long time before he said yes. I knew it was a hard thing, but it had to be done. Maman would never agree. It had to be secret until the very last moment.

Uncle Henri taught me what to do for the plane landing, and then we waited. If the mission was going to go ahead, the British would send us a coded message on the radio. That evening we tuned to the BBC. The Germans couldn't block the radio signals in the country as easily as they did in Paris. It was a clear, dry evening, and we could hear the announcer above the static. At 7:15 they played the notes that made up the Morse code for the letter *V.*

Then we heard a French voice.

"*Ici Londres.* This is London. Today is the one thousand two hundred and twenty-third day of the struggle of the French people for its liberation."

We listened to the war news, and waited for the messages for the Resistance. They came in the final minutes of the program. Most of them made no sense, but the radio operator for Uncle Henri's resistance cell had gotten our message earlier in the day.

"Pierre needs a new pair of pants."

"The cows in Belgium are yellow."

"Colette loves Philippe."

Finally, at the very end, we heard what we were waiting for: "The green bicycle has a flat tire."

That was our message. If it was repeated during the 9:15 broadcast, our operation was a go.

Mack got his things ready. I did the same,

slipping a rucksack on my back. One of Uncle Henri's friends was going to take in Maman, Charlotte, and me. We were supposed to meet him at the landing strip, and go home with him after the plane had taken off. We would hide with him until the Resistance could provide us with false identity cards—or so Uncle Henri thought. I had other plans.

At 9:15 Uncle Henri turned on the radio again. The war news hadn't changed in the past two hours, but that wasn't what we tuned in to hear. We needed to hear our message.

Once again, we heard a string of nonsense messages. The cows in Belgium were still yellow, but Colette had fallen out of love with Philippe. Someone's mission was off. Would ours be canceled as well? Then we heard it: "The green bicycle has a flat tire."

The plane had already taken off from England and was on its way. It was time for us to do our jobs.

"Let's go," my uncle said.

Mack caught my eye and nodded. I ran over the details of our secret plan in my head. Everything had to go perfectly.

Maman and Aunt Jeanne hugged good-bye.

Aunt Jeanne gave Charlotte a big squeeze too, and wrapped her arms around me for a moment.

My uncle pulled her away. "There's no time," he hissed.

He grabbed his flashlight and handed an extra one to me. "Remember to do it how we practiced," he said.

"I will," I assured him.

We crept out into the night. The moon was nearly full.

"A perfect night for flying," Mack said.

I wondered how the pilot would know where to find us, but my uncle had explained that the location had been radioed to London days ago. The RAF flew over, photographed the area, and gave it a code name. The pilot had to fly low to avoid German radar. That meant his radar equipment didn't work, and so a full moon and clear sky were the most important things. The pilot found his way by following landmarks.

"No landing site can be used twice," my uncle had said. "The *boches* turn up if you do that. They're like cockroaches, turning up everywhere."

We set off in a sprint across the fields. Mack carried Charlotte. Then we crossed a road, listening hard for German patrols, and dashed into the next field. About fifteen minutes later, we were in the tree line next to another field—the makeshift landing strip. I saw other shadowy figures in the trees.

"Green!" one of them said in a harsh whisper.

"Bicycle," my uncle responded.

Each new person to arrive was greeted with the code word *green* and answered with *bicycle*.

Mack was told to stand behind us until the plane was on the ground. My uncle asked me to translate, and I repeated his words exactly so that Maman would not get suspicious.

"Wait until they've unloaded the cargo and then you climb on," I said. "You must be fast. You'll only have a few seconds."

Mack winked at me. "Gotcha."

I leaned forward and whispered to Maman. "Stay close to Mack," I said.

She didn't question me but only nodded. Did she suspect?

We waited and waited. I began to think the plane wasn't coming after all. I heard a dog bark, and then other dogs joined in. Were they part of a German patrol? Had we been betrayed? No one else seemed to be concerned, and eventually the dogs quieted down. The next thing I heard was the distant drone of a plane. It was coming!

It got closer and closer. The roar of the engine was so loud I was afraid it would draw the entire German army to us. My uncle gave the signal and we rushed out onto the field with our flashlights. I stumbled and nearly dropped mine, but I made it to the edge of the landing strip. We stood in two straight lines.

When the plane was just above us, Uncle Henri flashed a Morse code signal with his light. The plane blinked a response.

"Lights," Uncle Henri said.

We shined our flashlights up into the sky, creating an L-shaped path for the plane.

The plane tilted sharply and came back toward us. It was just below the tree line when the pilot turned on his landing lights. The plane—a Lysander—touched down and bounced along our path. It took every ounce of courage I had not to drop my flashlight and run. I was sure the plane was coming right toward me. Instead it came to a stop next to Uncle Henri.

"Lights," Uncle Henri said again, and we turned off our flashlights.

The pilot turned off his landing lights and we were plunged into darkness again. In the light of the moon I saw people climb out of the plane. Then the two spies who were returning to England scrambled up the ladder. Uncle Henri stepped aside and motioned for Mack to follow them. This was when our secret plan kicked into place. Mack picked up Charlotte and walked to the plane. Maman ran after him, as I knew she would.

I saw the look of surprise on the pilot's face when Mack set Charlotte down on the edge of the plane and shoved Maman up the ladder. Then I saw the stricken look on Maman's face when I stepped back into the darkness, making it clear that I was not joining her.

"No!" she screamed, reaching out for me. She moved as if to jump off the edge of the plane but there wasn't time. The engine roared to life and the plane began to rumble across the field. In the darkness I saw someone grab her arm and pull her back.

I had thought about it and thought about it, but there was no way I could have gotten on that plane with them. Together, Maman and Charlotte would take up the space of one man. There wouldn't be room on the plane for me. Besides, I was the reason that Mack was going to have to take his chances crossing the Pyrenees instead of flying back to England. I had to make sure he got to Spain—and into British hands—safely.

I stood there listening until I couldn't hear it anymore. An owl hooted in the stillness, and then Uncle Henri and Mack pulled me toward the trees.

The other *résistants* had already disappeared into the night. I had waited too long. It was dangerous.

The trees blocked the moonlight, and I was glad that Uncle Henri and Mack couldn't see my tears. I was already lonely for Maman and Charlotte. Soon they would be with Papa in England. Georges—if he was still alive—was in Germany. And I was alone in France. Would I ever see my family again?

I wanted to run, to put as much distance between us and the landing strip as possible, but Uncle Henri put a hand on my arm. "Slow and steady. Nothing suspicious." He glared at Mack and then at me. "You have a lot of explaining to do," he said.

★ CHAPTER TWENTY-THREE ★

Étienne Michaud

Uncle Henri led Mack and me down the road. In the distance we heard a motor cough to life. Uncle Henri held his hand up for us to stop while he listened. One car on the road after curfew could be the doctor. Two or more meant Germans. My stomach filled with dread when another engine started, and then another.

"Quickly," Uncle Henri whispered. "Quickly."

The engines grew louder. We ran by the side of the road, ready to drop to the ground and hide when they got close. Uncle Henri led us underneath a small bridge. We crouched in the stream below while three German trucks crossed overhead. They stopped not too far away.

The patrol jumped from the trucks and called to each other in German while they searched the field. Our feet were soaked. Mack shivered in the cold water, and I worried he would get sick again. Suddenly we heard a shot. I tried to stand, ready to run, and hit my head on the low bridge. Uncle Henri winced at the noise and motioned me to crouch again.

Someone shouted and then we heard laughter and what sounded like teasing. Uncle Henri put his hand over his head and wiggled his fingers. A soldier must have shot at a rabbit and missed. A few minutes later, they got back into their trucks and drove off. We waited for a good five minutes, all three of us shivering now, and then jogged the rest of the way to the farm where I was supposed to hide with Maman and Charlotte.

Uncle Henri's friends, a man of about sixty and his wife, opened their door to an American man and a French boy instead of a mother and two children. Their clothes were old and patched, and the woman kept wrapping her hands in her apron, but they didn't let on how frightened they must have been to have an enemy pilot in their home. They greeted us warmly.

Uncle Henri was less pleased. "What were you thinking?" he asked.

"Maman and Charlotte will be safe," I said. "They'll be with Papa in England. Mack understands. He's willing to take the risk."

"I couldn't get on a plane knowing that Madame Durand and her daughter were in danger," Mack said.

I translated for him.

Uncle Henri shook his head. "And what is your plan now? A boy wanted by the Gestapo and an American pilot. You'll be shot on sight if you're caught. And anyone who helps you."

"I know the danger," I said. "I'm going to find a way to get Mack to the Pyrenees. I'll go with him to England. We'll set off in the morning. I'll take my chances with my identity card."

"Bah!" Uncle Henri said. "You won't leave until I can get you the false papers I promised." Then he put his hands on my face and pulled me to him, staring into my eyes. "When did you get to be such a man?" he asked.

I shrugged, secretly pleased at his words.

Mack looked from my uncle to me and waited for an explanation. "How much trouble are you in?" he asked.

"Some, but Uncle Henri knows deep down that we did the right thing. As soon as he can get those false papers for me, we'll leave for Spain. Tonight we'll stay here. Tomorrow, I don't know."

The farmer and his wife led us to the table and we had a simple meal. Then Uncle Henri slipped out into the night. "I'll be back when I have some news," he said.

Mack and I spent the next week or more in an underground cellar. I lost track of days in the dark. Mack and I told each other the plots of our favorite movies to pass the time. The farmer's wife brought us food when she could.

Finally, Uncle Henri arrived with a new student identity card. I had a ration card too. It took some time for my eyes to adjust to the daylight, but I saw that the forgeries were perfect. My new name was Étienne Michaud. I memorized it, along with my new birthday. I was pleased to see that Étienne was fourteen, instead of thirteen. He was born in Bordeaux, the first stop on our journey to the Pyrenees.

Uncle Henri waggled his finger. "The Nazis paid me a visit," he said with a chuckle. "They were full of questions about your cousins in Orléans."

The concierge must have handed over the postcard. "Was there trouble?" I asked.

"I don't know anything about your cousins in Orléans. I believe they are distant relations of your *maman*," Uncle Henri said with a wink. "How could I help them find you?"

"My plan worked," I said.

Uncle Henri nodded. "But they'll keep looking. The longer you stay here, the more likely you are to get caught. I've found some people who can do what you need," he said.

We looked at Mack's silk map while he explained our route.

"You'll take the train to Paris tomorrow—Sunday—and then transfer to a night train to Bordeaux. Take the local train, not the express. The *boches* are watching closely, but most of their checks take place on the express trains."

I translated for Mack.

"You and your friend have the same new last name," Uncle Henri pointed out. "You are father and son. Traveling to Bordeaux to visit family."

"Okay," I said. "What next?"

"You will arrive at Bordeaux at daybreak. Go directly to the hotel across the street from the train station's main entrance. Tell the night clerk that you are there to visit your aunt Simone Blanc. Remember that name. The clerk will answer, 'I went to school with her in Bayonne. I know her well.'"

I translated for Mack again. "What if there's more than one clerk?" he asked.

"That's why you must get to the hotel before eight o'clock when the day clerk takes over," Uncle Henri said. "If you arrive later, find something to do until nighttime. Nothing that will draw attention to you."

I nodded and tried to appear as calm as Mack did, but inside, my heart was hammering against my chest. The idea of going back to Paris was frightening all by itself, but once we reached Bordeaux, we had to trust strangers. What if one of them turned out to be a German spy, like Bob Jackson? Still, I was relieved to have to spend only one more night in that dark cellar.

I watched Uncle Henri make his way across the field, back to his own farm, and wondered if I would ever see him again.

★ CHAPTER TWENTY-FOUR ★

A Reward of Ten
Thousand Francs

November 1943

The next morning, the farmer and his wife kissed our cheeks, filled our rucksacks with bread and cheese, and wished us good luck. I would have liked to go to Uncle Henri's and Aunt Jeanne's to say good-bye, but I had already put them in too much danger.

I was reminded of how much danger when we arrived at the small train station. A Nazi command was nailed to a post: "All men who aid the crews of enemy aircraft will be shot in the field. All women who do the same will be sent to concentration camps in Germany."

But that wasn't all. The Germans offered a reward to anyone who turned in aviators and their helpers. "People who capture airmen or who contribute to their capture will receive up to ten thousand francs."

Mack saw me reading the poster and raised his eyebrows in a question. I shook my head. We couldn't speak in public, and the danger wasn't something he needed to be reminded of. I was frightened enough for both of us.

I bought our tickets to Paris and a farming magazine for Mack. The train was crowded, as it always was on Sunday, but we managed to find seats across from each other. Mack buried his head in his magazine and pretended to read. Soon the car was packed with passengers going back to Paris after the weekend, their bags full. Even if the *boches* wanted to come through to check papers, there was no room for them.

We arrived in Paris, and I planned to use my old trick of walking through the café. The Germans must have caught on. There was a checkpoint directly outside the street exit. I motioned Mack to a table, ordered two coffees, and waited. Fifteen minutes later, when most of the crowd had passed through, they packed up and left.

Mack pulled a pencil out of his pocket and wrote on the corner of a page in his magazine. "Follow behind?"

Mack would follow me at a short distance the way he had on that first day, when I had picked him up at the train station. That made sense—if one of us got arrested, the other could still go free. I ripped off the corner of the page with the English writing and rolled it into a little ball. "*Oui*," I said. "*Oui*."

I paid our bill. "*Au revoir*," I said to him, and walked to the door.

Mack followed a minute later. I crossed the street and headed for the *métro* the way I had so many times before. Suddenly I felt a pang of such sadness for Jacques that I had to stop and catch my breath. There was no time for tears now, but I was filled with despair. Had he been shot, or was he in a concentration camp? I made a promise to him in my head. *I'll keep the flame alive. I won't stop fighting until the Nazis have been defeated, or I'm dead.*

I wanted to take the subway to our apartment and ask the concierge what she knew, but I couldn't. I was Étienne now, I told myself. Michael was wanted by the Gestapo.

I tried to shake off my sadness while I waited

for the subway. Mack was a few feet away from me on the platform and we entered the same car through separate doors. There were two *boches*. I stood with my back to them and kept an eye on Mack. When we neared our stop, I moved in front of the doors. Mack did the same.

We made our way into the *Gare d'Austerlitz* without any run-ins with the Nazis. Mack stayed at a distance, but followed me toward the ticket window, where I bought two third-class tickets for Bordeaux. The night train was hours away, and I wasn't sure what to do. The movies were too dangerous after my last experience, and the train station was full of German soldiers. I finally decided to walk around the neighborhood until I came up with a better plan.

We were on our way out of the train station when I saw my old friend Pierre. He was on the sidewalk in front of the station. He wore his Young Guard uniform, as did the boy with him. I stopped so suddenly that Mack banged into me.

My eyes were locked on Pierre's and his on me. Mack hovered behind me, and I saw Pierre note his presence. He had to know that Jacques had been arrested and that I was on the run. I waited for him to blow a whistle or yell for a Nazi so he could collect his ten thousand francs. He stared at me for a long minute and then he nodded.

Stunned, I nodded back. Then Pierre took the other boy by the arm and led him away. Just before he turned the corner, Pierre turned back and waved.

My eyes filled with tears. I thought my good friend was lost to me forever, but he had just saved my life. I immediately thought of Jacques and wished I could tell him.

"*Ça va?*" Mack whispered.

"*Oui. Ça va,*" I answered.

Seeing my old friend reminded me that the streets of Paris were dangerous for me. What if Stefan was nearby too? He would turn me in in a second, even without the promise of a reward. I led Mack around the corner and back into the train station through another entrance. I also gave up the idea of the two of us pretending to be strangers. According to our papers, at least, we were father and son.

"Papa," I said. "Let's find a bench to wait. It's cold outside and I'm tired."

Mack didn't understand anything other than the simplest French words, but he understood "Papa." I took his arm and drew him to an empty bench. Every hour or so there was a rush of passengers, arriving in Paris from points south. Mack and I would mix in with them, careful to avoid checkpoints, and make our way to another bench. My eyes were constantly darting around the station, searching for danger. By the time our train arrived, I was exhausted.

We found seats in a crowded carriage. Mack kept his face buried in the French farm magazine. I looked out the window and watched Paris disappear behind us. *I'll be back if England and America win the war,* I told myself. *No, not if—when—they win.*

★ CHAPTER TWENTY-FIVE ★

Aunt Simone

Uncle Henri warned me that the main rail lines were swarming with Nazi soldiers, Gestapo agents, and suspicious train conductors—all of them on the lookout for downed aviators. The slow local trains weren't as closely watched.

Our car was stuffy. Mack opened a window, but soot and cold air rushed in, making us even more uncomfortable, and he closed it again. The stale air, the motion of the car, and the worries of the day all combined to send me into a deep sleep. I barely woke when the train stopped and started again. Passengers got off and on, but Mack and I stayed put.

At one stop, I heard German voices. Soldiers stomped onto the train, slamming their way from car to car. "Papers," they demanded. "Papers."

Some of them used the word *please*, but there was no politeness in their tone.

I whispered to Mack as quietly as I could. "Pretend to be asleep."

He threw his arm over his eyes and let out a loud snore while I handed the Nazi our papers, blinking as if I was barely awake myself. He glanced at them and moved on.

We arrived in Bordeaux at daybreak, showed our papers at the checkpoint, and found the hotel directly across the street. We walked up to the desk and I asked for a room. The clerk opened the registration book and I lifted the pen to sign Étienne Michaud's name.

"We're here to visit my aunt Simone Blanc," I said.

The clerk barely blinked. "I went to school with her in Bayonne. I know her well," he answered. Then he closed the book without registering our names, and took a key from a cubbyhole on the wall behind him. "Room 419. I'll let your aunt know that you've arrived safely," he said. "I'm sure she'll be here soon. In the meantime, I will bring you breakfast from the café."

My stomach rumbled at the mention of the word *breakfast*. Mack and I had finished our bread and cheese sometime over night. I didn't know how much money we would need along the way, and was afraid to spend any of the little bit we had. "Thank you," I said.

The room was small and grim with windows facing the stone wall of the building next to us. I was glad I could not see the street, and the Nazis marching up and down. A few minutes later, there was a quiet knock on the door. "Breakfast."

Fake bread and fake coffee never tasted so good. The clerk was off duty now, and eager to practice his English on Mack. We were just finishing our meal when there was another knock on the door.

"I know your aunt Simone," said a man's voice. "I went to school with her in Bayonne."

The desk clerk nodded and I opened the door. A small man rushed in. "*Bonjour, mes amis,*" he said. "Hello, my friends." He kissed my cheeks and then rushed over to Mack to do the same. "Call me Philippe. I'll lead you on the next leg of your journey."

As always, Mack asked about his crew. I saw the look of disappointment cross his face when Philippe didn't recognize the names. I saw something else too—a feeling I had come to know well—guilt.

"We wait for two more packages on tonight's train," Philippe said, "and then off we go."

"Can't we leave today?" I asked.

"Your friend will be safe here tonight. There are too many aviators waiting to get out and not enough guides," he explained. "We have to bring a few at a time. Not just one. But you can go back to Paris on the next train. You don't have to wait."

"Back to Paris?"

"Yes," he said. "We have guides to take your friend the rest of the way."

"I can't go back," I said. "I have to go to England."

Philippe shook his head. "It's no journey for a boy," he said. "You have to climb steep mountains, cross a river, evade German and Spanish patrols.

It's too difficult. Besides, what will you do in England?"

"My family's in England," I said. "My father is working with General de Gaulle. They're expecting me."

"No one told me about you, only about the aviator," Philippe said with a shrug. "These Basque guides, they're very difficult. I don't think he'll agree to take you."

I started to panic. If I didn't go with Mack, what would I do? My family was gone. My friends were arrested. "I have nowhere else to go," I said, my voice cracking with fear. "The Gestapo is looking for me. I have to go."

Mack heard the alarm in my voice. The clerk and I both talked at once, translating for him.

"I won't go without Mi—" Mack cut himself off. "Without Étienne," he said.

The clerk translated for Philippe. The two men left the room. We could hear them arguing in the hall, but I couldn't make out the words. Mack put a hand on my shoulder. "I mean it," he said. "I won't go without you. If we have to, we'll cross the mountains alone. I have my map and a compass. We'll make it."

I knew crossing the mountains without a guide

would be nearly impossible. "Thanks," I croaked. "We'll work something out."

The door opened. The small man threw his hands up in the air in surrender. "Go," he said to me. "Go. But be prepared for the Basque to turn you away."

★ CHAPTER TWENTY-SIX ★

Nighttime Confessions

Mack and I spent the day in our room, never talking above a whisper. When he arrived at work that evening, the desk clerk brought us some thin soup and more bread. I would never get used to this dry, wartime bread. It was half straw.

He told us to sleep while we could. "The hike over the Pyrenees is difficult," he said.

I tried, but I couldn't sleep. I lay there in the dark and worried about what Philippe had said about the Basque guide. Would he leave me behind?

Mack was awake too. "You should have gotten

on the plane with your mother and Charlotte," he said. "You'd be with your father by now."

"I don't want to face my father," I blurted. I didn't know I felt that way until the words came out of my mouth. But it was true. Uncle Henri could have found someone to guide Mack. I didn't have to stay behind. I didn't want to see Papa's face when he heard the story of Georges's arrest.

"Why?" Mack asked.

I could only just make out his outline in the dark. He rolled over to face me.

"My brother is in a German prison camp because of me," I confessed.

Mack listened to my story. "You can't blame yourself," he said.

"I pulled the shirt from Georges' uniform out of the trash," I said. "That's how the Nazis knew he'd come back to Paris. They saw his shirt on my bed and searched the building. They found Georges in the basement. If he's dead—" I cut myself off.

"Don't you think that the Nazis would have searched the basement even if they hadn't seen the uniform?" Mack asked. "Didn't they search the whole block?"

Mack was right—the Germans were nothing if not thorough. But I still felt as if it was my fault they searched so hard for Georges. "I've been trying to make it up to Papa and to Georges by being a *résistant*, but then I put Maman and Charlotte in danger too. If Georges doesn't come back, I don't think my father will ever speak to me again."

"I can't believe that's true," Mack said.

"It is," I answered. "My *papa* was never much interested in me. Georges was his favorite."

"Favorite or not, how could your father be anything other than proud?"

I didn't answer.

"What do *you* think about what you've done for France?" Mack asked. "Are you proud of yourself?"

The question surprised me. I measured every action I took against what I believed Papa would think. I never stopped to consider how I felt. The words were slow in coming. "I am," I said finally. "I'm proud of what I've been able to do for France. I helped a lot of aviators leave Paris."

Mack nodded. "You escaped when your friends were arrested. Your mother and sister are safe in England because of you," he said. "I'm safe because of you. You're brave and you think fast on your feet. Your *papa* will see that."

I sighed. Tears pricked at the back of my eyes. I remembered the times I felt brushed aside by Papa, the times he and Georges went off on their adventures. Papa only included me when he had no choice.

"My *papa* doesn't value me in the same way he values my brother," I said. "If one of us has to die, he'd much rather it be me." Those were terrible words to say out loud, but I believed they were true.

"I value you," Mack said quietly. "All the American soldiers you helped escape value you. But that doesn't matter, really. Real value comes from inside," he told me. "Be proud of yourself. Know that you're smart and brave. No one can take that away from you, not even your father."

Could I value myself if Papa didn't value me? Didn't love me? I tucked Mack's words away to think about another time. "Why won't you talk about what happened to your plane?" I asked. "My other aviators couldn't wait to tell me their stories."

Mack sighed. He rolled away from me onto his

back. I was about to give up on ever hearing his story when he began to speak. The words were halted at first, then stronger.

"We had engine trouble," Mack said. "I should have turned the plane around and headed back to England, but I thought the engine might come around. I fell out of formation. We were like sitting ducks for the Luftwaffe." He shook his head. "I should have tried to put her down. I might have been able to land in a field."

"What did you do?" I asked.

"I waited too long. The Luftwaffe was on us, and we got hit. I gave the order to bail. I was the last one out. My men were scattered all over. There were German soldiers on the ground, shooting at the parachutes. I should at least have given the order to bail out before we were hit—given my men a chance."

"It's not your fault," I said. "You wanted to carry out your mission."

"I waited too long." Mack stared at the ceiling. "Maybe some of them got away," he said. "Maybe."

★ CHAPTER TWENTY-SEVEN ★

A Bike Ride

Shortly after daybreak the desk clerk arrived with breakfast and two more aviators. David Brooks from England and Jerry Underhill from Virginia. Philippe was right behind them. He handed us each a train ticket to a town called Dax.

"*Boches* all over," he said in broken English. "We go to Dax and then ride bicycle." He asked me to translate the rest.

"Leave the hotel one at a time, a few minutes apart and go directly across the street to the station. Don't stand together on the platform," I said. "When the train comes, we'll get on two different cars—Mack and David will follow me on the first one. Jerry is with Philippe."

We hadn't had time to share our stories, but I saw the surprise in Jerry's and David's eyes when they learned that I was going too.

Philippe continued with his instructions and I translated. "When you get off the train, leave the station and walk down the lane to your left. There's a shed about fifty meters away. Wait behind it."

I left the hotel a few minutes behind Philippe and waited on the platform. Mack was a couple of minutes behind me; David and Jerry followed. I learned about what good manners the English had when David got on the train. He stepped on a woman's foot.

"I beg your pardon," he said, clear as a bell.

I froze, waiting for someone to yell.

The woman only smiled and moved over so he could sit. The other passengers pretended nothing unusual had happened. It was like all of France had joined the Resistance.

The rest of the short train ride was uneventful. There wasn't even a Nazi checkpoint in Dax. I followed Philippe at a distance and trusted the others to do the same. When we had all gathered,

Philippe opened the shed and wheeled out old, broken-down bicycles. I wondered if the threadbare tires would survive the trip.

"Dangerous now," Philippe said. "Ride in twos, far apart. Me alone in front." He pointed to David and Jerry. "You next."

That left Mack and me to take up the rear. We set off about fifteen minutes behind the others. "Do you know where we're going?" Mack asked.

"No idea," I told him. "South." I knew that was the smart thing—if Mack and I got picked up, we couldn't tell the Nazis where to find the others, but I hated not knowing where we were going. We were on country roads with little traffic. A couple of times we came to a turnoff and didn't know where to go. Then I learned to look for Philippe's signals. On one signpost he had chalked a *V* in the right direction. At another, he tucked the handkerchief he wore around his neck under a rock.

We rode and rode, not daring to stop and rest. The wind turned our cheeks red. My fingers felt frozen to the handlebars. Finally, late in the afternoon, we came upon Philippe fixing his front tire. He said nothing, only nodded his head slightly to the left. We turned into the farm lane. We saw the other bicycles just inside a barn and wheeled ours in behind them.

David and Jerry were slumped on the floor, rubbing their legs. My own muscles twitched. I remembered the day I had to ride away from the Gestapo, how I had pedaled all over Paris. Today I was even more tired.

Philippe arrived a few minutes later. We never saw the people in the house, but Philippe went inside and came out with a rich country stew. The men organized a schedule to keep watch and I crawled into the hay, searching for a warm place to sleep.

The next morning we set out again. It was another long, cold ride and we were getting closer to the mountains. The rolling hills were hard on our tired legs and we fought against wind from the ocean. My legs went numb and my mind drifted. By afternoon I wasn't sure if I was awake or dreaming.

Mack and I reached a little house on the outskirts of the village of Saint-Jean-de-Luz. Philippe stood outside, chatting with a woman. He nodded around back and we wheeled our bicycles behind the house. Inside, our hostess greeted us with soup and bread. It was warm in the little house, and once my stomach was full, my mind drifted again. I was hardly aware of the conversation around me. At one point Mack stood me up and walked me to a pallet in another room and I slept.

When I woke, Philippe was gone. Our nameless hostess explained what would happen next. "We will mix with the people going to market in the village," she said. "There's a bridge at the bottom of the hill with a German checkpoint. You all have papers, yes?"

Everyone nodded.

"Mix with the crowd. The Germans will hardly look at you," she said. "Then follow me—not in a bunch, but in a single file."

David and Jerry were nervous. Mack and I were used to passing through German checkpoints by now, but they had only been in France for a few days. I was the first to follow our hostess. Mack offered to take up the rear. We rounded a corner and suddenly there was the Atlantic. I had smelled the salt air all day yesterday, but I hadn't seen the ocean since before the war began. I took a deep breath and mixed with the villagers crossing the bridge. A *boche* waved me on without even checking my papers. I crossed the bridge and leaned against a wall, pretending to knock a stone out of my shoe.

David and Jerry were too close together and they kept looking at each other. David handed over his papers, but Jerry tried to slip through the checkpoint without showing his.

"Halt!" a guard yelled.

Jerry took a step back and raised his hands like they did in American cops-and-robbers movies.

"Idiot!" I said under my breath.

David walked toward me, panic in his eyes. I cocked my head in the direction of our hostess and he followed her.

The guard was looking at Jerry's papers and saying something. Jerry stared back with a blank expression. I ran up and scolded him in rapid French like he was a toddler.

"I'm sorry," I said to the guard. "My cousin isn't right in the head since the war. I lost track of him for a minute."

The *boche* stared at me through narrowed eyes. I knew Jerry couldn't understand my words, but maybe the guard didn't speak French either. I raised my finger to the side of my head and made the sign for cuckoo. "He got shot in the head," I said.

The guard dropped the papers into my hands

as if Jerry's injury was contagious and waved us on. I took Jerry's arm and dragged him off the bridge.

Mack ambled along behind us. In his country clothes and flat beret, he fit right in. I held on to Jerry and walked up the narrow, cobblestoned street our hostess had taken. She was lingering at the top of a hill. When she spotted me, she turned a corner. Then she slipped into the side door of a house. Jerry and I did the same. Minutes later, Mack arrived.

We were greeted by a young Belgian woman who introduced herself as Tante Liberty. "We're expecting your Basque guide this afternoon," she said. "He'll lead you over the mountains and into Spain, and then contact the British consulate there. The British will take you by car to Gibraltar, and then back to England."

"How long will it take?" David asked.

"You'll be in Spain by morning."

"Spain and then England," David said with a sigh.

Tante Liberty nodded. "Your guide is Basque. He speaks the Basque language and only a little French, so you won't be able to talk. He's made many trips over the mountains and he's never lost a flyer. Trust him."

"Philippe said there were arrests," I said.

"Not on the trek over the Pyrenees. Here in France." Tante Liberty's face clouded. "My father," she said flatly. "Many others. We've lost many guides and two safe houses. There's a bottleneck of aviators trying to get out of the country, and not enough guides to lead them."

"My comrades in Paris were arrested," I said. "I only just got away."

"You've got to get back to England and fly those airplanes of yours," Tante Liberty said, turning to the aviators. "Drop your bombs. Hitler has to be defeated."

CHAPTER TWENTY-EIGHT

Climbing the Pyrenees

I agreed with Tante Liberty. "Yes," I said to the aviators. "Hitler has to be defeated."

We were all silent for a minute, then Mack asked what we could expect on our hike.

"It will take all night and you'll be following goat tracks and smugglers' paths," she warned. "The Bidossa River between France and Spain is tricky—sometimes ankle-deep, sometimes waist-high or even higher. You'll be tempted to celebrate when you cross it, but don't. Spain claims to be neutral, but their leader, Franco, is a fascist just like Hitler. The Spanish police, the *Guardia*

Civil, arrest escaping aviators and hand them over to the Nazis. You won't be safe until you're in British hands."

"When will we leave?" I asked.

"As soon as it's dark," Tante said. "Get some sleep. I'll wake you as soon as Florentino arrives."

I listened to the men's snores and finally dropped off myself. The next thing I knew, Mack was shaking me awake. "He's here."

The four of us walked down the stairs and found a craggy, dark-skinned Basque man in the kitchen. He was using a small knife to cut sausage and cheese. He ate right off the blade and washed everything down with wine. When he finished, he motioned to the rest of us to eat too.

We were nearly done when he threw some shoes into the middle of the table. They were rope-soled and tied with ribbons.

"Alpargatas," he said. He wore a pair himself.

"These are best for hiking in the Pyrenees," Tante Liberty explained. "They grip the mountain paths and water runs right out of them."

"They don't look like they'll hold up," Mack said.

Tante Liberty smiled. "They won't. You'll bring an extra pair."

I put mine on. They were big, but they would certainly be quieter and easier to walk in than my wooden *sabots*. Florentino hung a second pair around my neck with a nod. I smiled at him with relief. He wasn't going to leave me behind. But it turned out that Florentino wasn't the one to worry about.

"Wait," Jerry said. "You think you're coming with us?"

"Of course he's coming with us," Mack said. "His family's in England."

"Don't you think a kid is going to slow us down?" Jerry asked. "I haven't come all this way to get arrested because of a kid."

"A kid saved your neck on that bridge this morning," Mack said. "He's been risking his life for months to get people like you and me back to England, and now the Gestapo's after him."

Jerry looked away and grumbled something under his breath to David.

Mack slammed the table. He remembered to use my new name, not the name of the boy the Gestapo was searching for. "Étienne and I are going with Florentino. You two can wait and go another night. But I don't know who will save your life the next time you do something stupid."

David shook Jerry off. "I'm with you," he said to Mack.

Jerry glared at us, but he sat down to strap on his *alpargatas.*

"No trouble," Florentino growled in French. He stepped out into the night.

Tante Liberty gave us each a walking stick and our instructions. "Single file," she said. "Don't talk. Don't make any noise at all. Stay close. If you fall behind, you'll be left behind," she warned.

Jerry looked at me with a satisfied expression. It was like he wanted me to be left behind.

"There could be Germans anywhere," Tante Liberty continued. "Follow Florentino's orders. I'll see you after the war."

She kissed all of us on both cheeks and then we stepped out into the night.

Florentino walked quickly up a hill and across the main road. Jerry followed. Then David. Mack motioned me to go next. He would bring up the rear.

The night was damp and chilly, and soon it started to rain. We followed a country lane through winding hills. We skirted a small village and I smelled suppers cooking over kitchen hearths and listened to goats in a nearby meadow.

Soon we climbed over a livestock fence and the route got steeper. We inched along a path that seemed to lie between two vineyards. I could see only the faintest of shadows in front of me, and I learned to rely on my ears to find my way—the slap of a branch against a face or an arm, the clank of a goat's bell, a stumbling foot.

My clothes were completely soaked. The *alpargatas* didn't slip and slide on the wet path the way my *sabots* would have, but the pair around my neck got heavier and heavier. I could feel a shoelace digging into my neck. My soggy rucksack weighed me down too, and I considered leaving it on the path for someone else to find. I was afraid if I slowed down to take it off, I would lose track of the others. The night was so black I couldn't tell if my eyes were open or closed.

All the while we were climbing, climbing, climbing. I wasn't used to the thin air at such a high altitude. It seemed like I couldn't fill my lungs. I huffed and puffed, afraid my loud breathing would give us away to a Nazi patrol.

Sometimes we'd reach what seemed like the top of a peak, and I'd breathe a sigh of relief, thinking we were halfway there. But then we'd round a hairpin turn and the track would get even steeper. Sometimes the path edged along sheer cliffs. I was grateful for my walking stick, but I often had to use my other hand to grab the cliff's side and pull myself up. Once I grabbed a rock and it came loose under my grip. It plunged off the side of the track and I nearly went with it. It was a long time before I heard it hit the ground. I got down onto my knees and crawled until the path widened again.

My legs were so tired that all I could think about was putting one foot in front of the other. I think I might have fallen asleep on my feet. I guess I slowed down, because suddenly Mack was behind me. He lifted my rucksack and my spare *alpargatas* off my back and added them to his burden. For a few minutes there was sweet relief, but then the pain set in again. My soggy pants chafed against my thighs and they burned with each step.

Finally, we reached the top. I nearly banged into Florentino. Jerry and David were sprawled on the wet ground. I joined them and waited for Mack.

David patted me on the shoulder. "Good job," he said.

"Shush!" Florentino warned in a harsh whisper.

It was a shock to see the lights of Spain below

us. France had been in blackout since the war began. I had forgotten that there were places in the world where people could turn on their lights without having to worry about bombs dropping on them.

When Mack joined us, our guide passed around bread, cheese, and milk. We accepted it silently until Jerry suddenly swore. "Goat's milk," he said, spitting it out.

That earned a harsh curse from Florentino. "Leave behind," he warned in French.

I didn't bother to translate. I plugged my nose and drank. I didn't like goat's milk either, but my body needed fuel to keep going.

We didn't rest for long. Florentino gave us each a couple of sugar cubes to suck on for energy and checked our shoes. We changed into our spare *alpargatas,* and then we set out again.

I dreaded what was coming next. Crossing the river into Spain would be the most dangerous part of our journey.

★ CHAPTER TWENTY-NINE ★

The Lights of Spain

I kept my eyes trained on the lights of Spain. The trek downhill was so steep that often we found ourselves jogging. I would have fallen many times without my walking stick to slow me down. Every once in a while the clouds lifted and the moon came out. It made the path easier to follow, but I was scared to cross the river in the moonlight.

The hike to the bottom was faster than the hike up had been. Suddenly I heard rushing water. The Bidossa River! My feet were blistered and I thought the cold water would feel good. I was about to step forward when Florentino signaled us to stop. He crouched in the underbrush a few feet from the river, listening.

A few seconds later, over the sound of the river, I heard voices. German voices coming from the Spanish side. In the moonlight I saw a patrol march across a bridge not too far away. Their voices carried in the cold air. A car followed them across the bridge, its lights shining on trees. Nazi swastikas fluttered from either side of the hood.

We waited until the sounds were long gone.

Finally, Florentino crept down to the riverbank and waded into the center of the rushing water. The water came up to his waist, and I realized that for me it would be chest-high. When he came back to us, his expression was grim.

"Too high," he whispered in French. "Current strong."

I translated for the others.

"Is there another way to cross?" Mack asked. "A bridge?"

Florentino shook his head. "Patrols." He took off his pants, tied the legs together, and slipped them over his head. "Do like this," he said.

"He wants us to make a chain," I explained.

The rest of us tied our pant legs the way Florentino had, slipped them over our heads, and held on to the trousers of the man in front of us. David held on to Florentino's pants. I was linked to Jerry. Mack was linked to me.

The moon and the clouds must have been on our side, because just then it went dark again. Florentino started toward the riverbank.

When it was my turn, I stepped into the water. I was wrong about it feeling good on my feet. It was icy torture. The water reached my knees, my waist, and then my chest. The current was tugging at me, trying to pull me downstream, and the rocks underfoot were slippery. I used my walking stick to keep my balance, but the current seemed to be pushing harder and harder. I needed to go slow, but Jerry was rushing. He banged into David, and David slipped with a noisy splash.

We all stopped for a moment while David found his footing, and then started again. I stepped into a hole and suddenly I was under the water. My stick was ripped out of my hand, but I tried hold on to Jerry's pants while the water crashed around me. I hoped he would be able to pull me up. Instead, there was a violent tug in the other direction. Jerry had ripped himself out of my grip. I fell backward, deeper into the water.

I tried to swim to the surface. My head was above water for a second. I gasped for air. I wanted to yell for help, but I was afraid that would draw the Germans to us. Seconds later I was pulled under again. I could feel the water dragging me downriver. I fought against it, trying to get my footing. My arms flailed around, searching for something to hold on to. My lungs were ready to explode The pants against my neck were strangling me. And then they weren't. Mack had lost his hold on me.

I was alone. I was exhausted. I didn't know which way was up. Fighting the current seemed to make things worse. For one second I thought about letting go completely. My limbs went limp. I felt peaceful, resigned. Then I remembered my promise to Jacques to keep the flame alive. I even thought I heard someone whistle our V-for-Victory signal—three short toots and one long whistle. I was too close to freedom to give up now.

I dug my feet into the riverbed and pushed myself up with a rush of energy. Mack was there to catch me. He held on to the back of my jacket. The water was chest height. Together we fought to stay upright in the middle of the river while I gasped for breath.

A few minutes later Mack put his walking stick in my hand and we took careful side-by-side steps. I don't know how we made it, but soon the water was around my knees again, and then my ankles, and finally I reached the Spanish side of the riverbank where Florentino was waiting. I collapsed into his arms and he lowered me to the sand. David crouched next to me and rubbed my arms and legs, trying to warm them.

Mack flew at Jerry. "You left him to drown!" He remembered to whisper, but I could tell he wanted to yell.

Jerry edged away. "What was I supposed to do? Let him pull me under too?"

"You should have helped him," Mack spat. "Coward."

Florentino came between them. He put his hand to his lips to indicate quiet and then pulled Mack away, over toward me. They ran their hands up and down my arms and legs to make sure I was okay. I had scrapes from the rocks in the riverbed, but I hadn't broken anything. I was cold and sore, but I was alive.

We rested for a few minutes and then tugged our wet pants over our wet legs.

There was a faint light nearby—a Spanish guard

shack. Florentino used hand signals to tell us to stay away from it. He passed around hunks of cheese. Then—too soon—he set off again. One by one we crawled through the bushes and then up an embankment to a set of railroad tracks. Florentino crossed them, crouching to stay low. Jerry was next. He stumbled over the tracks and fell hard, hitting his face. His angry curse was as loud as a gunshot.

Dogs barked in the distance and a bright light suddenly illuminated the tracks. A door opened, and I heard running.

Florentino froze, then slipped into the darkness on the other side of the tracks. He might as well have been on the other side of the mountains. There was no way to reach him without being seen.

I lay flat in the bushes, silently cursing Jerry. He got to his feet and tried to run, yelling for Florentino. A shot flew over my head, and then another. And then I heard a scream. Jerry had been hit.

★ CHAPTER THIRTY ★

A Final Decision

Jerry clutched his leg and rolled from side to side on the tracks just above me, cursing. I hugged the embankment.

Two Spanish guards ran right past me and stood over Jerry. One move and I would be spotted. I heard what sounded like a kick and Jerry screamed again. They shouted questions at him in Spanish while he shouted at them in English.

"I have American money," he said over and over again. "I can pay."

I clamped my teeth together to stop their chattering and pressed my face into the dirt while

I tried to flatten myself against the ground. I was sure that the guards would see me. Instead they had some kind of an argument. My Spanish wasn't all that good, but it seemed like one of them wanted to search for more Americans, while the other said they couldn't leave Jerry alone or he would escape.

Then, the very thing that had made our hike and the river crossing so difficult saved us. A light drizzle turned into a steady downpour. After another burst of conversation, the guards made a decision. One of them took Jerry's feet, and the other his shoulders. Carrying him between them, they walked back toward their guardhouse.

A minute later, the light went out and Florentino was at my side. "Quickly," he whispered. "Quickly." He led us over the railroad tracks, and we set off at a slow run. I put Jerry out of my mind and focused on keeping up with the others.

The river had given us the cruel idea that we were nearly at our destination, but the rest of the journey seemed to take hours—up a cliff, up and down foothills, around some ruins, and finally, at daybreak, we staggered down a hill toward a Spanish farmhouse.

There was smoke coming from the chimney

and I could smell food. The promise of safety was one thing, but food—food! I would have broken into a run if my legs could do such a thing after hiking all night. Instead I hobbled into the kitchen with the others. An old woman greeted us—her face melted into a mass of wrinkles when she smiled.

There were basins of warm water to soak our feet . . . and food. Such food! I hadn't seen so much in one place since before the war—sausage and ham and eggs and cheese and mouthwatering corn bread and hot milk. Goat's milk, which I drank only to be polite, but all of the other delicious flavors wiped the taste from my mouth.

The old woman smiled, watching us eat. The men of the farm came in and watched us too, all grinning. There was a little boy, around Charlotte's age. He peered into my face, laughing, and flapped his arms like a bird. "Pilot?" he asked in English.

I laughed too. "No," I said. I was about to say I was just a boy, but instead I told him what I really was. "Soldier," I said.

Mack caught my eye and nodded.

I sat a little straighter. I was a soldier, as much as any of the men around the table. And I was proud of that. I was sorry we had lost a man, but that wasn't my fault. Florentino said Jerry would probably end up in a German POW camp. I worried about how much damage Jerry would do to the escape line. How much did he know, and would he talk to try to save himself?

One of the farmers spoke French, and I asked him about the other Americans and Englishmen who had come through. "Many, many," he told me. "But not so much now. No guides."

I nodded. We had heard that all along the route—the Nazis had broken the escape line and the Resistance was struggling to put it back together. How many aviators were stuck in France waiting for someone to bring them to safety?

Florentino left to call the British consulate from a telephone in the village. David praised me for keeping up on the hike and I thanked him politely, but his opinion and his praise weren't what was important. I wondered if that's what Mack meant by true value coming from the inside. I knew I had done my job and done it well. It didn't matter what anyone else thought.

The aviators napped, but sleep wouldn't come to me. So many thoughts swirled through my head—pride in the fact that I had kept up with the men and made it safely over the mountains, sadness that Jacques was not with me, and fear for the aviators who were left behind in France.

There was a time when I would have longed to tell Papa all about my trek over the mountains while I desperately waited for his praise. I had carried his disapproval on my back like a heavy rucksack ever since Georges was arrested. But I had put down that burden on the mountain last night and started to trust in my own value.

By the time Florentino returned, I had made a decision. I found the French-speaking farmer and asked him to translate. Florentino propped his head in his hand while I shared my plan. He agreed, nodded tersely, and curled up for a nap.

When Mack woke up, I told him that a car would arrive shortly to pick up him and David and take them to Gibraltar. From there they would fly to England. Then I handed him two letters. One was for Maman. The other for Papa.

"I'm not going with you," I told him. "I'll rest here for a couple of days. Florentino's going back tonight, but he'll be here again before the end of week. I'm going back to France. I want to help rebuild the escape line."

"Is it because you don't want to face your father?" Mack asked.

"No, not anymore. This is different. I have to be able to face myself."

Mack tried to tell me that I had already done enough, but my mind was made up.

"You're the one who told me that value comes from inside," I said. "I have to do this. I'm a soldier. You fight your war from the sky, but I have to fight mine on French soil."

Mack's eyes misted over and he pulled me into a hug. "I'll make sure your parents get the letters," he said. "I'll tell your father about how brave and strong you've been."

"Thank you," I said. I still wanted Papa to be proud of me, but I was doing this for me, not Papa. If I was going to look myself in the eye after the war, I had to stay. And, like Mack said, that was more important than any praise Papa could give me.

My imaginary ladder, the one I had built rung by rung, was strong enough to carry me through the rest of the war—until France was again free.

★ HISTORICAL NOTE ★

Michael and his family are fictional characters, but the things that happen to them are based on real-life events. By the end of 1941, thirty-eight countries were involved in World War II. Many of the countries in Europe, including France, were occupied by Nazi soldiers who tried to control everything about the day-to-day lives of the occupied people.

From the moment the Germans marched into France, the French people faced hardships. Food was the biggest problem. Bread and meat were rationed almost immediately. Other foods were soon added to the list along with goods like leather, coal, fabrics, and soap. Food prices tripled between 1939 and 1943. The winters of the Occupation were among the coldest and snowiest on record, and fuel was scarce.

Regular German soldiers, the Wehrmacht, kept order. But along with Hitler's army came the secret state police—the Gestapo. The Gestapo's job was to hunt down and kill anti-Nazis.

Most of the French people focused on getting enough food and fuel to stay alive. Others did what they could to defy their new rulers. They refused to speak to German soldiers, gave them the wrong directions, and wrote anti-Nazi slogans on walls and German posters. As the war continued, the behavior of the Nazi forces became increasingly brutal. More and more French men, women, and children joined the Resistance.

There were at least a hundred different resistance groups

in France alone during the Second World War. Some focused on spreading information via underground newspapers. Other spied for the Allies or sabotaged German factories and communications. Still others formed a kind of underground railroad to keep Allied aviators out of Germany's hands so that the soldiers could make their way back to England and continue to fight the war.

To reach England, the aviators first had to make a dangerous journey across France and hike over the treacherous Pyrenees mountains into Spain. Once they reached Spain, the English could transport the men to Gibraltar—a small British territory on the southern tip of Spain—and then relocate them to England.

Historians estimate that civilians rescued as many as six thousand aviators who were shot down over the Netherlands, Belgium, and France. By 1943, the escape lines had become so good at their work that Allied airmen had a 50 percent chance of making their way back to England.

It's impossible to know just how many ordinary people risked their lives to help these men. Some provided food, shelter, and clothing. Others created false papers and identities for them, and still others—like Michael, Jacques, and François—took on the dangerous job of leading the men across France and into Spain.

As in the novel, some of the escape lines were infiltrated and destroyed by Nazi spies, but the Resistance groups rebuilt the lines again and again.

Security against the Resistance became more and more ferocious as the war continued, especially after the German army began to suffer losses in North Africa and the Soviet Union. Some historians estimate that for every Allied soldier who made his way back to England, one French, Dutch, or Belgian helper lost his or her life. Men who were caught faced a firing squad. Women were sent to concentration camps, where many died.

These rescuers knew that they were risking their own lives to save strangers. They did it because they believed in the same cause—freedom.

After years of great sacrifice all over the world, the Allies won the war in 1945.

CHILDREN'S ROLES IN
★ THE FRENCH RESISTANCE ★

Children had to grow up quickly during World War II. The children of France, and those in other occupied countries, were cold and hungry. Many had fathers and brothers who were killed, missing, or prisoners in Germany. Jewish children in Europe faced an even bigger problem. They were rounded up and sent to die in concentration camps.

Anyone who fought back against the Nazis risked prison and death. Still, for people who believed in the cause of freedom, the risk was worth it. Some of those people were children.

Although most of their names are lost to history, one sixteen-year-old boy named Jacques Lusseyran started a resistance group in Paris made up mainly of teenagers. The incredible thing was that Jacques was blind.

Other children got involved in the Resistance through their parents or their older siblings. The Germans didn't suspect them, so moving around was easier for children than it was for many adults. Teenage girls and young women often pretended to be on innocent walks with their boyfriends when, in fact, they were leading Allied soldiers to safe houses or train stations. Boys often acted as couriers and guides, passing information from one resistance operative to another, spying on the Germans, or leading downed aviators along the escape routes to Spain.

They were ordinary children who did extraordinary things in the face of great danger. In refusing to accept defeat, they kept the flame of resistance alive.

★ HISTORIC CHARACTERS ★

Some of the characters in Michael at the Invasion of France, 1943, *were real people who played a part in* World War II.

Charles de Gaulle fought in the First World War under Marshal Philippe Pétain. He was wounded and captured at the famous Battle of Verdun and tried to escape from German prison camps five times. In the early days of World War II, de Gaulle led a failed attack against the invading Nazi troops before escaping to England. From London, he urged the French people to resist the Nazis and then became the leader of the Free French Forces. After the war, he served as French president from 1958 to 1969.

Adolf Hitler, the German dictator, led the Nazi Party and served as chancellor of Germany from 1933 to 1945. Once he won control within Germany, Hitler prepared to take over the rest of Europe. He also blamed all of Germany's problems on the Jewish people. His leadership led to a world war and to the deaths of nearly six million Jews. When it became obvious that Germany would lose the war, Hitler took his own life on April 30, 1945. Germany surrendered to the Allies a week later.

Henri Philippe Pétain was France's greatest hero in World War I, for which he was made a marshal of France—an officer of the highest rank. In June 1940, he became the prime minister of France and asked Hitler for an armistice. He modeled his government in the Free Zone after Hitler's fascist regime and was notorious for collaborating with Germany. Pétain's government passed anti-Jewish laws and deported Jews to German concentration camps. After the war, he stood trial for treason and was sentenced to death. Charles de Gaulle commuted the sentence to life in prison, where Pétain died in 1951.

Franklin Delano Roosevelt, the thirty-second president of the United States, led the nation out of the Great Depression. The American people resisted involvement in the war, and Roosevelt tried to keep the country out of the conflict. But when Japan bombed naval bases at Pearl Harbor, America was forced to fight. The United States declared war on Japan, Germany, and Italy. Roosevelt partnered with the leaders of Great Britain and the Soviet Union and was a strong commander in chief. He died of a stroke a month before Germany surrendered. Before he died, he cleared the way for peace, including the establishment of the United Nations.

★ TIME LINE ★

World War II lasted for almost six years and involved thirty-eight countries on five continents. The time line below outlines some of the key events of the war in Europe.

1938

March   Nazi Germany announces its Anschluss, or union, with Austria. German troops march into Vienna.

1939

March 15   Germany, which had annexed the Sudetenland area of Czechoslovakia the year before, seizes the rest of the country.

September 1   The Nazis invade Poland from the west with a new type of warfare—a *blitzkrieg*, or lightning war.

September 3   France and Great Britain declare war on Germany.

September 5   The United States declares that it will remain neutral.

September 17   The Soviet Union invades Poland from the east.

September 27   Poland surrenders. Germany and the

Soviet Union agree to divide the country between them.

1940

April 9	Nazi troops invade Denmark and Norway.
May 10	The Nazi *blitzkrieg* sweeps across the Netherlands, Luxembourg, and Belgium. German troops enter France.
May 15	The Netherlands surrenders to the Nazis.
May 24	The Battle of Dunkirk begins. British and French forces appear to be cut off, but over the next nine days more than three hundred thousand soldiers manage to avoid capture by the Nazis in a famous evacuation using fishing boats, yachts, lifeboats, and anything else that could float.
May 28	Belgium surrenders to the Nazis.
June 3	German bombs fall on Paris's airports.
June 13	The French government, desperate to protect the art, architecture, and history in Paris from German bombs and tanks, announces that Paris is an "open city," which means they will not defend it.

June 14	German soldiers march into Paris at dawn. By midmorning, huge German flags fly from every public building.
June 16	Marshal Pétain becomes the new French prime minister. The next day he announces that he has asked Hitler for an armistice.
June 18	From the BBC radio station in London, General Charles de Gaulle asks the French people to resist the Nazis.
June 22	The armistice agreement between France and Germany is formally signed in the same clearing in the Compiègne Forest where Germany surrendered at the end of World War I. The agreement cuts France in two. Germany occupies the north and the entire Atlantic coast. This is called the Occupied Zone. The south, led by Pétain's new fascist government, is called the Free Zone.
June 23	Pétain's government charges General de Gaulle with treason and sentences him to death.
September 17	The French people are ordered to line up for ration cards, which are issued

according to age. Food and other goods
are harder and harder to buy.

September 27   Germany signs a pact with Italy and
Japan.

1941

April 6   The Nazis invade Greece and Yugoslavia.

April 17   Yugoslavia surrenders to the Nazis.

April 17   Greece surrenders to the Nazis.

June 22   Germany invades its former ally the Soviet
Union.

July 12   Great Britain and the Soviet Union form
a military alliance against Germany.

August 31   Radios belonging to Jews in the Occupied
Zone are confiscated. Soon they will lose
their bicycles and their telephones too.

December 7   The Japanese bomb Pearl Harbor in
Hawaii.

December 8   The United States, Great Britain, and
Canada declare war on Japan.

December 11   Hitler declares war on the United States.

May 29	All Jews in France ages six and up are ordered to wear yellow stars on their clothing, embroidered with the word *juif,* or Jew.
July 16	French policeman round up thirteen thousand Jewish refugees in Paris for transport to concentration camps.
November 8	U.S. and British forces land in North Africa.
November 11	Germans invade the Free Zone in the South of France, taking control of the entire country.

1943

February 2	German generals surrender to the Soviets at Stalingrad. It is the first major defeat of Hitler's army.
February 16	All French men between the ages of twenty and thirty-four are ordered to go to Germany to work for the war effort. Many of them slip quietly away to join the Resistance instead.
May 12	The United States and Great Britain

achieve a major victory over Germany in North Africa.

July 9   British and American forces begin the invasion of Italy.

September 8   Italy surrenders to the Allies.

October 13   The new Italian government declares war on Germany.

1944

June 6   D-Day. Just after midnight, Allied paratroopers land in Normandy. At dawn, German lookouts spot Allied ships off the coast of Normandy while planes thunder overhead. The invasion of France begins.

August 17   Most of the Nazi soldiers in Paris retreat in what Parisians call "The Flight of the Fritzes."

August 20   Hitler sends an order to destroy Paris, but Paris's German commander refuses to burn the city.

August 25   French and American soldiers march into Paris. The German commander surrenders.

August 26	General Charles de Gaulle leads a victory march down the Champs-Élysées.
December 16	In a last desperate attempt to turn the tide of the war, Hitler's forces attack Allied troops in the Ardennes forest in Belgium. The Battle of the Bulge begins.

1945

January 25	The Battle of the Bulge ends with an Allied victory.
April 30	Adolf Hitler commits suicide.
May 7	Germany surrenders.
May 8	V-E, or Victory in Europe, Day. The German army officially surrenders in Berlin.

★ GLOSSARY ★

Allied Powers or Allies: The name given to the countries that opposed Germany and the other Axis Powers. In World War II, those countries included Great Britain, the Soviet Union, and the United States.

armistice: An agreement by opposing sides in a war to stop fighting. A truce.

***arrondissement*:** Paris is divided into twenty *arrondissements*, or neighborhoods.

aviator: A pilot, copilot, or anyone else with a job to do on an airplane, including gunners and bombardiers.

Axis Powers and Axis: Germany and the countries that fought against the Allied Powers in World War II, including Japan and Italy.

***blitzkrieg*:** A sudden military campaign intended to bring about a fast victory. Lightning war.

***boche*:** An insulting French word for Germans, especially German soldiers. Its origin is unclear, but it may be a shortened version of alboche, a combination of the French words for German (*allemand*) and blockhead (*caboche*).

***ça va*:** A French phrase that is both a question and an answer. It means both "How's it going?" and "It's going fine."

collaborator: A person who worked with or helped the Nazis. The slang word for a collaborator was *collabo*.

concierge: The caretaker of an apartment building or a hotel.

curfew: A rule that demanded people stay indoors, usually at night.

democracy: Government by the people.

extinguish: To destroy or put something out, especially a fire.

fascism: A government that insists on obedience to one all-powerful leader.

goose step: A type of military marching in which the legs are not bent at the knee.

*gendarme***:** The French word for policeman.

Great War: World War I.

*Kommandantur***:** The German word for commander's office.

Luftwaffe: The German air force.

*métro***:** The Paris subway system, or underground train.

munitions: Military weapons and ammunition.

Nazi: A member of the Nazi (National Socialist German Workers) political party, which was led by Adolf Hitler.

newsreel: A short film about current events that was shown before the feature film in a movie theater.

*nom de guerre***:** A secret code name used during wartime.

occupation: The capture and control of an area or country by a military force.

propaganda: Misleading information used to support a cause or point of view.

refugee: Someone who has been forced to leave his country to escape war or mistreatment.

résistant **(male) or** *résistante* **(female):** The French word for someone who worked in the Resistance, a person who struggled against the Nazis.

sabot: A wooden shoe, or clog.

sabotage: To destroy or damage something.

swastika: The symbol of the German Nazi Party.

Third Reich: The popular name for Germany while it was governed by Adolf Hitler and his Nazi Party.

verboten: The German word for forbidden.

★ FURTHER READING ★
Want to learn more about the World War II?
Here are some great nonfiction sources.

DK Eyewitness: World War II by Simon Adams, published by DK Children, 2007. Photographs, illustrations, documents, and maps tell the story of the people, places, and events of the Second World War.

The Good Fight: How World War II Was Won by Stephen E. Ambrose, published by Atheneum, 2001. Photos, maps, and personal stories outline America's involvement in World War II.

Hitler Youth: Growing Up in Hitler's Shadow by Susan Campbell Bartolctti, published by Scholastic Nonfiction, 2005. Have you ever wondered about what it was like to live in Germany under Hitler? This book tells the story from the viewpoint of kids and teens who were there.

In Defiance of Hitler: The Secret Mission of Varian Fry by Carla Killough McClafferty, published by Farrar, Straus and Giroux, 2008. Varian Fry, an American journalist, helped more than two thousand refugees escape from Nazi-occupied France.

You Wouldn't Want to Be a World War II Pilot!: Air Battles You Might Not Survive by Ian Graham, illustrated by David Antram, published by Franklin Watts, 2009.

Acknowledgments

First I have to thank two authors I've never met: Peter Eisner, who wrote *The Freedom Line: The Brave Men and Women who Rescued Allied Airmen from the Nazis During World War II*, and Sheri Green Ottis, author of *Silent Heroes: Downed Airmen and the French Underground.* Their books provided me with research and real-life stories I could never have duplicated on my own. Any mistakes or inaccuracies in Michael's story are, of course, my own.

Deepest thanks go to the members of my writing group, Josanne LaValley and Kekla Magoon, for their close readings and especially for their warnings when I let the story lag. And, of course, to the friends who let me name my fictional American aviators (even the unlikable ones!) after their husbands.

As always, I want to thank the editorial and design teams at Dial for their careful attention, especially Andrew Harwell and Rosanne Lauer.